3024

TIME FOR CHANGE

1977: William Cobridge has sold the factory and taken early retirement, but his wife Paula can't help but feel that something is still missing from her life. She wants to move to a smaller, more modern house, but knows that Nellie, her mother-in-law, will never accept the change. In fact, Nellie isn't really coping with anything at the moment . . . Meanwhile, William and Paula's daughter Sophie is sharing a flat with her Aunt Bella, who is exasperating both as her flatmate and boss at work — and Sophie wants out . . .

CHRISSIE LOVEDAY

◆

TIME FOR CHANGE

Complete and Unabridged

LINFORD
Leicester

First published in Great Britain in 2016

First Linford Edition
published 2016

A catalogue record for this book is available
from the British Library.

ISBN 978–1–4448–2912–9

Published by
F. A. Thorpe (Publishing)
Anstey, Leicestershire

Set by Words & Graphics Ltd.
Anstey, Leicestershire
Printed and bound in Great Britain by
T. J. International Ltd., Padstow, Cornwall

This book is printed on acid-free paper

1

Paula sighed deeply. She felt thoroughly fed up with her life and wanted something to change, she thought as she looked round the large kitchen and put the saucepan with the potatoes on the stove to cook. She planned to broach the subject of moving house again to her husband, William. Now that there were only the three of them living there, Cobridge House was far too large for them. Nellie, her mother-in-law, was always going to be the major problem. She didn't want to move, and now she had reached seventy-five, felt herself well established here.

Paula heard William come in and went out into the hall to greet him.

'Hallo love,' he said, kissing her cheek. 'How are you?'

'Same as usual.'

'That bad, eh? Anything in particular?'

'Not really. I just feel particularly fed

1

up today. Your mother's been very difficult. She wanted me to start cooking dinner at about three o'clock. She seemed to think I was a servant. I don't know where that's come from.'

'Oh, I'm so sorry, love. I'll go and talk to her.'

'It's this enormous house that gets me down. If we could only move to somewhere smaller and modern.'

'I suppose we'll have to discuss it with her again. But you know what she's like. Won't even consider it.'

'Maybe you and I should move on our own. That'd certainly show her.'

'How could we?'

'Oh, I'm not being serious. Of course we couldn't go without her. I'm just feeling weary, I suppose. I'll go and finish supper now. Half an hour?'

'Thanks. I'll go and see how she is.'

Paula went back to her preparations. She had a casserole and a fruit crumble in the oven. She plonked some carrots in a pan. No doubt Nellie would dislike something in the meal and moan about how times had changed. They still had Mrs Evans coming in to clean each day, for which Paula felt grateful. She went through to the dining room and set the table. It seemed ridiculous to eat in such a large room, but Nellie liked it and was used to doing it each night. At least she settled for lunch on a tray in the breakfast room.

By the time William came down with his mother, dinner was ready. He sat her down in the dining room and poured her a drink.

'Is Cook bringing the food in?' Nellie asked.

'Paula's bringing it,' he said.

'I suppose she's planning to eat with us. I see she's laid three places.'

'Of course she is.' He gave up. It was pointless trying to explain yet again to his mother that Paula was his wife of well over twenty-four years.

'Here we are,' said Paula cheerfully, carrying the tray of food in. She didn't really feel as cheerful as she sounded, but felt determined not to have another long session of arguments.

'What have you cooked for us today, dear?' asked Nellie.

'A nice beef casserole. I think you're going to enjoy it. Shall I serve you with vegetables?'

'No, I'll help myself. I think I can manage to do that. How's Bella getting on?'

William was slightly thrown by her question. Bella, his much younger sister, hadn't been spoken of for ages. She was living in a flat in Leicester with their own daughter, Sophie.

'Haven't heard for a while,' he said. 'I suppose she's all right.'

'And how is the factory getting on?' Nellie asked.

William paused again. They had sold the factory almost seven years ago. Since then, he had taken early retirement; and though he'd looked for another job, he had never found anything that really suited him. He'd done some consultation work, enough to pay him well, and spent a lot of time on the golf course.

'Do you remember we sold the factory?' he said to his mother. 'We sold it to a large company who paid us reasonably well.'

'I hope they did. And I'd like some carrots, please.'

Paula exchanged glances with her husband. This was so typical of the conversations they had together. Nellie had forgotten so many things, and seemed to leap from topic to topic. 'If you pass me your plate back, I'll put some out for you.' She smiled at the woman, though she felt ready to murder her. William had no idea what she went through each day.

'I can help myself,' snapped Nellie.

'I'll pass them to you,' William said.

'You do it,' his mother ordered. He did as she said, and she then moaned she hadn't got enough. When he tried to put more on her plate, she told him off for overloading it.

'Make up your mind,' he said, trying to be patient.

The meal went on in a similar way through the pudding. At last they were all finished, and Paula made coffee. She muttered to William that they needed to discuss moving and so he broached it.

'This house is much too large now, Mother. We were thinking it might be a good time to sell it and move to somewhere more modern. A smaller house, even a bungalow. We could afford a nice place, in the country maybe. What do you think?'

'Move? Oh no, don't be silly, dear. How on earth would we live somewhere small? There wouldn't be enough room for all the staff. Where are they, by the way?'

'They've all gone, remember?' he said. 'There are only the three of us. We have so many empty rooms, it's ridiculous.'

'One needs space around,' Nellie said grandly. 'One needs to have plenty of room.'

'We could buy somewhere with space,' Paula put in. 'Somewhere we'd all have room to move without all the old-fashioned furniture around us all the time.'

'You're being very silly, dear,' Nellie admonished her. 'I've lived here all my life, with my husband and his parents. I don't think I knew their parents, but they lived here too. I couldn't possibly condone moving.' She actually sounded quite logical in the end.

William looked angry. He wanted to move and knew full well that Paula did too. They could easily sell this place and get a lot of money for it. A housing developer might like to buy it for a start. It could easily be turned into flats, and there was loads of space outside in the garden for more houses. He remembered his own childhood with a pang, and the large family gatherings they'd had. Perhaps it was time to organise another one, though it would all fall on Paula. No cook to do all the work or maids to serve the food. Maybe it wasn't such a good idea. If they ever did persuade Nellie to give her consent, they could have another family party as their goodbye.

'I think I need to do some work now,' Nellie said. 'There are some designs I really need to finish before tomorrow. Will you see to the cups, Paula, dear?'

'Of course.'

'Tell Cook I enjoyed dinner this evening. Thank her, will you?'

'Of course,' repeated Paula stupidly. Still, what was the point in arguing? If Nellie wanted to believe they still had a cook, who was she to say anything to disillusion her? 'Good night. Can you manage all right?'

'Of course I can. I'm not stupid. Don't forget to let the cat out,' Nellie threw behind her as she sailed out of the room.

'Oh good lord,' Paula muttered. 'We haven't had a cat in years. Even then, it lived in the kitchen and Cook let it out. Do you think she'll be all right? Do you need to go and see her?'

'I'll leave her for a while,' William said. 'I'll check on her later. Do you want some more coffee?'

'I don't think so.'

'Then come here and sit beside me,' William invited her. She rose and snuggled into the armchair with her husband. 'That's better,' he said. 'Now, what are we going to do about Mum and moving?'

'Lord knows. You can see how it is. She still thinks we've got the factory and a staff of hundreds. Well maybe not hundreds, but you know what I mean. I'm going slowly bonkers here with her all day. I was seriously thinking of getting someone to come in and look after her and even go back to teaching.'

'Could you still do it?' William asked her. 'Teach, I mean.'

'I don't see why not. It would be marvellous to get out of this depressing place.'

'It's something to think about. But it's a long time since you did anything in the teaching line.'

'Maybe. But I was a good teacher in my time. Except Bella, of course. But there always are limits.'

'You didn't do too badly,' he said.

'Gosh, do you remember when she ran away from her boarding school?'

'Could I ever forget? She always was a difficult child. Doesn't seem to have changed all that much now. According to Sophie, she's still a nightmare.'

'How is Sophie? Doesn't seem long since she was just a little one going off to school. How old is she now?'

'Oh really, William. Twenty-three. Mind you, you'll be fifty on your next birthday.'

'And so will you the next year. Wherever does time fly to?'

'I'm not sure it was such a good idea for those two to share a flat,' Paula mused. 'I gather things are a bit dodgy. Sophie rang me yesterday. She sounded rather fed up.'

'Really? Why?' William was losing interest in her words and had picked up the paper.

'I don't want to bore you, dear.'

'Hmmm?'

Paula gave up and cleared the cups away, took them into the kitchen, and washed up. William might have helped, she thought. She would have liked to sit and read the paper, too, but the dishes needed doing and breakfast needed setting out ready.

Could she go back to teaching? She would need to do quite a bit of work to catch up. So many new things had come in, and there were always different things to learn. As long as Nellie could be looked after, and well, there was also William. Without the factory, he seemed to be at a bit of a loss. Forty-nine was far too young to be retired, but what else could he do? Perhaps he might find a job as manager somewhere. It would certainly be an improvement on the golf club. She wasn't even sure he got the exercise usually given by a golf course. She suspected he spent a lot of time in the bar with anyone who was willing to chat to him.

She tipped the dirty water away and wrung out the dishcloth, then picked up a tea towel and began to dry the dishes. How they'd taken it for granted, having someone to do all these chores. Oh, she'd always looked after herself and William when they were first married; but since his father's demise, they'd moved downstairs to be with Nellie. Their own dear little flat was shut away and neglected, along with what had once been the staff bedrooms. It all seemed so ridiculous, having so much space and nobody living there. Sophie and Bella both had rooms as well, in case they wanted to come back for a weekend or stay for a holiday. Bella was most unlikely to come back, but Sophie came regularly. Paula thought about her daughter and wondered whether to phone her. She decided against it and went back into the lounge and to William.

He was slumped in his chair, fast asleep. The paper had dropped to the floor and he was snoring gently. Paula smiled and picked up the paper as silently as possible. She sat down and began to read it. Suddenly there was a shriek from upstairs. It was a blood-curdling sound that scared her half to death.

'William, wake up. Your mother's . . . well, there's something wrong. Come on.'

He got up, staggering slightly, and the two of them went upstairs to see what was wrong.

'Whatever is the matter, Mother?' William asked when they got to her room.

'It's your father. He's missing. I looked in his wardrobe and everything's gone. All his clothes, everything. Even his brushes are missing. What's happened to him?'

'Oh Nellie,' said Paula gently. 'It's all right.'

'Dad is dead, Mother. He died many years ago. You've got to stop doing this. It's frightening for Paula.'

'What do you mean? How can he be dead? He was here yesterday.'

'He wasn't,' William told her. 'You were dreaming.'

'Dreaming? I can't possibly be dreaming. I saw him and we went to bed together. Didn't we?'

'No, Nellie,' Paula said. 'He died over twenty years ago. Look, I think we need to call the doctor. Tomorrow I'll phone him and get him to come and see you.'

'That's a good idea,' William agreed. 'Now, Mum, let's get you back to bed. Try to sleep, and we'll see how you are tomorrow.'

'Tomorrow. Yes. I think he may come back tomorrow.'

They helped her back into bed and Paula tucked her in. She felt sorry for the woman, but also irritated. It was difficult to live this situation, especially when it was with someone who had always been so dominant in their lives. If it had been her own mother, she was thinking, would she feel so very different? Her mother and her aunt had both died in the past five years. Paula really missed them both.

'Good night,' she said quietly, closing the door.

'Good heavens,' William said once they were both in the hall. 'She really is getting beyond a joke.'

'I know. She's really gone downhill in the past few weeks. Perhaps the doctor will be able to make some suggestions. Will you be around in the morning?'

'I suppose I could be. You think he'll come in the morning?'

'I'm sure if I ask him he will. He's looked after your mother for many years. There must be some medication she can have.'

'I might think about going to bed myself. I feel pretty weary,' William suggested.

'It is ten o'clock. Not sure where the evening went. You'd better go and make sure the doors are all locked.'

He went downstairs and checked that everywhere was secure. They were both right, he thought. The house was far too large and cumbersome for them. He made up his mind to go to the estate agents the next day and see what they had on their books. His mother would just have to put up with it. The way she was behaving, she would be muddled wherever she was.

2

It was already well after eight o'clock. Sophie was anxious about her flatmate. She went and knocked on her bedroom door and called out, 'Bella? Wake up. It's nearly time to leave.' She waited for a moment and knocked again. 'Bella, come on. I'm leaving in fifteen minutes.'

'Go away,' Bella moaned. 'Leave me alone.'

'You really should come now.'

'I'm dying,' came back the reply.

Sophie closed her eyes in despair. It was the usual tale. Bella had been out till very late and was now wanting to sleep off her hangover.

'Okay. Shall I call the funeral director now or wait till I get home again?'

'Just leave me in peace.'

'What shall I tell them at work?'

'Use your imagination. Now, please go.'

With a sigh, Sophie went to swallow her coffee, then quickly munched her toast and switched off all the appliances. If Bella did ever get up, she would make herself something to eat and eventually turn up for work very late. Why on earth should Sophie say anything to their boss? She hadn't seen her aunt this morning and was sick of making excuses.

Soon she was sitting on the bus, watching the morning Leicester crowds busying along the streets. The flat she shared with Bella was in a pleasant part of town, out towards the Stoneygate area. It was a short bus ride to their workplace, usually taken together. Bella's absences were becoming more regular, and it always seemed to be down to Sophie to make excuses for her.

'Morning Sophie,' said a couple of the ladies when she arrived.

'Morning,' she replied.

'No Bella today?'

'She'll be along later, I expect.'

'Another late night?' one of them asked cheekily.

'That's no way to speak of your boss,' Sophie said frostily. 'I think you know what you're doing today. Continue with the tops you were working on.'

She went into the office and sat down at her desk. It was a fairly small company that made exclusive clothes for some of the larger stores. Bella was the main designer; she was responsible for overseeing the cutting, and setting the girls to work on the various designs. The owner of the company did most of the selling and he then passed on to Bella his instructions for new pieces. Unfortunately for Sophie, Bella seemed very good at designing and managed to keep him happy most of the time. Sophie would have loved to do some designs herself and see the results in the shops. As it was, she had to be content with making her own clothes and using some of the offcuts for trimmings. She didn't often wear them for work as she felt guilty about taking the pieces of fabric home with her.

The rest of the staff arrived, and soon

there was the sound of sewing machines whirring and the crunching of scissors cutting out new fabric. They were a good team who all worked well together.

'No Bella today?' asked one of the cutters.

'Apparently not,' replied Sophie.

'Not well?'

'I really don't know. I'm assuming you have plenty of work? If not, I'll sort out something for you.'

'No, it's okay; we've got a load to do. I just wondered where the lovely Bella had gone. We always enjoy our chats, don't we, lads?'

'I'm sure you do.' Sophie knew exactly what they meant. She turned away from them and went back into the sewing room. Six ladies were working at the machines and all seemed to be well. She went back into the office she usually shared with Bella and shut the door. What on earth was she going to do? The boss had asked Bella for two new designs, and as far as she knew, they hadn't been done.

She looked in Bella's desk and in the drawers, but there was no sign of anything. She opened a folder and looked at the design brief. One item really appealed to her — a long evening dress using a lovely fabric from the stockroom. She picked up the description and began to sketch an outline shape: fitted waistline with floating panels down the back. She became engrossed in her work and soon had two views almost finished. Glancing up at the clock, she saw it was almost half-past one. She looked out into the workshop and saw the girls were all missing. They had gone outside for lunch.

Guiltily, Sophie pushed her designs into her desk and took out her sandwiches. She quickly munched them and threw the papers away. Then she went outside to fetch the ladies back and set them working again.

'Still on your own, then?' asked Mary, one of the older women who was still classified as one of the 'girls'.

'Indeed I am. How are you doing

with the shirts?'

'Not bad. Still got quite a heap of them to do. I reckon we'll still be doing them in another week.'

'Okay, as long as the quality is there. I'll look in later to check them.'

'Right you are, Sophie. Come on, ladies. Let's get back to work.' They all rose together and went back to the workshop and were soon busy again.

It was about three o'clock when Mr Hill arrived. He knocked on the office door and came in. 'No Bella today?'

Sophie hesitated. What could she say? 'No. I haven't seen her.'

'But you share a flat, don't you?' He sounded irritated. 'So where is she?'

'I think she wasn't feeling well this morning. I didn't actually see her, but she intimated that she felt ill.'

'Really, this is getting all too frequent. It's the third time in less than two weeks. Tell her she'd better buck her ideas up or she'll be out of a job. Has she made a start on any of the new designs?'

'I'm not sure. Shall I look?'

'If you know where. I'll be in my office. Bring them in to me if you find them; I want one of them made up quickly.' He left the room and disappeared into his own office next door.

Sophie fought a battle with herself. Should she take the design she'd been working on, or should she lumber Bella? Heavens, the woman deserved to lose her job, but Sophie knew she'd probably be the one to suffer if she did. She picked up her sheets of paper and took them into Mr Hill's office.

'I've found this one,' she said slowly. 'Is it one of the ones you wanted?'

'Yes. Oh, this is lovely. She must have been working on it yesterday. Can you work on the pattern for it? I need it in a size fourteen. I know it's outside your remit, but if you think you can do it, go ahead.'

'I'd love to. The blue fabric? The thin floaty stuff, and lined with deeper blue. It'll look stunning.'

'Yes indeed. You've got a good eye,

Sophie. Perhaps we don't need Bella after all. Though without her designs, I suppose we'd be lost.'

'I . . . yes, you're right of course.' She'd almost admitted to doing the design herself, but knew it would put Bella in an even worse light.

'You're a good girl. I'd like it ready as soon as possible. Get Mary to work on it. She's one of the best.'

'Right you are. I'll see to getting the pieces sorted and then get the cutters working on it. Anything else?'

'No, that's it for now.'

She went back to her office walking on air. Bella had done her a real favour being absent today. She didn't even mind her getting the credit for doing the design, as she was going to oversee the making-up of the dress. She worked hard for the rest of day and had about half the pieces ready by the time she went home. She couldn't stop smiling as she rode the bus back.

Sophie planned to phone her mother that evening and tell her about her success, assuming Bella would be out of the way of course. She also needed to ask after her grandma. Mum had sounded rather concerned about her the other day. She felt very hungry as she went along. She thought about supper and wondered what they might have. It was too much to expect that Bella would have prepared anything, so she called at the butcher's when she got off the bus.

'I'd like some minced beef please,' she asked the cheery man.

'How much?'

'Oh, sorry. Half a pound please.' He weighed it and she paid, picked up the package, and left the shop. She'd make a sort of pie out of it, and if Bella was out again she'd have the rest tomorrow. It would be typical of Bella to go out for the evening and decide she didn't want to eat. It made it difficult to know what to get each day. If Sophie didn't attempt to feed them both, her aunt would complain bitterly.

She found it difficult to think of Bella

as her aunt. There were only eight years between them, though Sophie was much more mature than Bella, who was slightly autistic. Not that anyone would have known it, as Bella was actually rather talented at her chosen career. It was her erratic behaviour that caused the most concern to her niece. She seemed to take no responsibility for anything she did.

With a sigh, Sophie entered the flat. 'Hi there,' she called. 'Anyone at home?'

'Oh, you're back. Good. Have you brought anything for supper?'

'Of course.'

'Thank goodness; I'm starving. There's nothing in the fridge, and the cupboard's virtually out of everything.'

'There's nothing to stop you going out to buy stuff,' said Sophie irritably. 'You're just as capable as I am of going shopping.'

'But you do it so much better than I ever could. I always buy the wrong things. So what are we having? For supper, I mean?'

'I've got some minced beef. I'm going to make a pie out of it with mashed potatoes on top.'

'Is that it? I fancied a couple of nice juicy chops or something.'

'Then go and buy them. This will keep till tomorrow.'

'I can't go out now. I'll just have to make do with your mince. Give me a call when it's ready. I'm going to have a bath now.'

'Yes, milady. No, milady. Three bags full, milady.' She muttered it under her breath so Bella didn't hear. Sighing, she went into the kitchen and started on their meal. When she'd made the pie and put it in the oven, she went along to her bedroom. She changed into her trousers and slumped down on the bed.

She was beginning to know how her mother felt about doing the cooking and generally being the dogsbody. It wasn't going to last, she decided. She'd tackle her flatmate and they would come to some sort of compromise. If Bella didn't want to cook, then she must take on the cleaning. After all, they were supposed to be sharing, and that meant Bella must take her share of the work as well. Her father had bought the flat for both of them, presumably using money from the business, so it didn't belong to just one of them.

'Going out now,' called Bella.

'What? I thought you were starving.'

'I called someone. He's willing to buy me dinner, so I'm going out.'

'What about the food I've cooked?' Sophie asked, coming out of her room.

'Chuck it.'

'You haven't even been to work today. You were dying, remember?'

'That was then. This is now. Don't wait up. I expect we'll go dancing after eating. Bye.'

'You really are the limit, Bella. It can't go on like this.'

'Yeah, whatever. See you in the morning.'

Fuming with anger, Sophie went into the kitchen and took her pie out of the oven. She served half of it onto a plate and sat down with a tray. It was actually very tasty, she thought, and soon finished her portion. She looked at her watch. It was almost seven o'clock. She wondered whether to phone her mother, or perhaps she might be in the middle of cooking their dinner. Hang it, she thought, and decided to call.

'Hallo, Mum,' she said into the phone. 'Is it convenient?'

'Hallo, Sophie,' Paula responded. 'I can snatch a few minutes. How are you?'

'Fed up. I was thinking I might come home for the weekend. Is that all right?'

'Course it is, darling. You're always welcome, you know that. What's wrong?'

'It's Bella. She's impossible. Never does anything, and seems to expect me to cook the whole time.'

'I know the feeling,' said Paula. 'So what has she done now?'

'Wouldn't go into work today, and now she's gone out. She expected me to cover for her. The boss is getting thoroughly fed up with her. Trouble is, she has talent and he likes her work.'

'Perhaps you just have to leave her to it.'

'I did a design yesterday and stupidly let him think she'd done it. Now I've progressed with it and left him thinking she actually put pencil to paper.'

'Oh well, I suppose it's too late for that one. Look, we'll talk when you come over at the weekend. I must go now. Sorry, love, but dinner's almost ready.'

'Sorry I chose a bad moment. I'll see you on Friday evening, probably quite late. Can you meet me at the station? I'll let you know the time when I've booked the train.'

'Of course. Take care, love, and don't worry about Bella. She's always been a pain.'

'You make me happy to hear that. Bye, Mum. Love you.'

'Bye, darling. Look forward to seeing you.'

Sophie sat down and turned on the television. There was nothing she wanted to see, and feeling somewhat bored, she got out her sewing. Soon she was wrapped in the creative process and realised she had quite enjoyed her evening. At ten o'clock she decided to pack it up and go to bed. She had just fallen asleep when she heard a crash, and shot out of bed. Feeling slightly alarmed, she slowly pushed open the door and called out, 'Who's there?'

'S' all right. Only me,' came back Bella's voice. 'Wanted something to eat.'

'I thought you were going out to dinner?'

'So did I.' She gave a loud hiccup. 'Sorry. Went to a club instead. No food there.' She hiccupped again.

'Seems as though there was plenty to drink though. You're somewhat inebriated.'

'Yes, indeedy. Inebri-whatsited. That's such a nice word, don't you think? Inebriwhatsited. That's me.' She gave a giggle. 'So what's there for me to eat?'

'There's the pie thing. You can heat that up. I'm going back to bed now. Try to be a bit more quiet.'

'You do it for me, love. I'm incapable of doing anything properly.'

'So I've noticed. I'll put it in the oven but it's up to you to look after it. Right?'

'Righty-ho. Yes, sir.' She saluted and slumped down on the sofa.

'You will look after it?' Sophie asked her doubtfully.

'Course I will. You go to beddies now. Get some sleep and don't forget to wake me in the morning.' She hiccupped again and slumped back on the sofa.

Sophie put the pie in the oven and brought the timer in to rest beside Bella. It would ring in about fifteen minutes, so should wake her up. She stared at the woman lying on the sofa looking completely out for the count. What on earth was she doing to her body, getting so drunk every night? It couldn't go on like this.

3

Paula told William and Nellie about her phone call over dinner. 'So she'll be home Friday evening. One of us will need to fetch her from the station.'

'I'll go,' William offered.

'Yes, well, we'll decide nearer the time.'

'Is Bella coming too?' asked Nellie. 'It's ages since we've seen her. She's my daughter, you know.'

'I don't think she's planning to come,' Paula replied. 'Sophie didn't mention it if she was.'

'Phone her and ask her.'

'She's out for the evening, or so Sophie told me.'

'Phone her. Tell her that her mother wants to see her.'

'I'll call her tomorrow. No use leaving a message.'

'I'll phone her myself if it's too much trouble.'

'It isn't that. Of course I'll phone her tomorrow, when she's home.'

'William, I want you to phone her,' Nellie insisted. 'This cook person is not willing to do anything for me.'

'Don't be silly, Mother. Paula has explained that Bella is out. There's no point in her phoning when she's not there, is there?'

'She may be back by now.'

'I doubt it,' Paula said. 'She's gone out for the evening. I don't think she'll be back before we all go to bed.'

'Oh dear. It's so long since I've seen her.' To their concern, Nellie began to sob silently. Tears poured down her cheeks.

'Come on now, Mother,' William cajoled her. 'I'm sure she'll come and see us all very soon. I'll phone her tomorrow and see what she's doing. Now dry your eyes, and Paula will fetch us some pudding.' He raised his eyes to his wife and she nodded, beginning to collect their plates.

Paula carried them into the kitchen and gave a sigh. Nellie was getting worse. The doctor had been that morning and suggested she might have an infection, so he had prescribed a course of antibiotics. It was surprising that it could make her so strange. Paula sighed again, deeply. It seemed that she would be expected to look after her mother-in-law for the rest of her life. She collected the dish of trifle from the fridge and carried it through. No doubt Nellie would complain there wasn't a proper pudding, as it was cold.

'Here we are,' she said as cheerfully as she could muster.

'What's that?' Nellie asked.

'Trifle. I thought it would make a nice change.'

'That's not a pudding. It's something you have for tea. For a party. Are we having a party soon? We haven't had a proper party in ages.'

'Perhaps we might,' answered William. 'It would be nice to have the family over, wouldn't it?'

'There's Joe and Billy and Lizzie. They could all come.'

'And their wives and children, maybe.' Paula smiled. It would mean a lot of work for her, but it would please them all. She was quite willing to throw a party if it meant so much to Nellie.

'If you're willing to do it, that would be great,' William said gratefully.

'On Sunday,' Nellie told them.

'I'll need a bit more time than that to organise it all. There are so many people to invite, with all the children and their husbands.'

'You're not alone, my dear,' Nellie said. 'The cook will do most of the work. You must organise the drinks, William. Must have beer in the sideboard, and make sure the cook knows about making cakes. I shall wear something new. Can we go and buy something smart for me, Paula, dear?'

'I expect so. It will be in a few weeks, you understand.'

'Yes, of course. Not next Sunday then. Sophie will be here, won't she? Pity Bella won't. She'll doubtless be out with her beau.'

'Possibly,' William said with a sigh. As far as he knew, Bella had a whole string of beaux, as Nellie called them. He had no illusions about his sister, who was twenty years younger than him. She might have been born on a different planet.

'Is she getting married soon?' Nellie asked. 'It's time she was married and giving me some grandchildren. I haven't got any yet.'

'You've got Sophie. She's your grandchild. Our daughter.' Paula had told her so often, but Nellie seemed to forget.

When they had finished eating, Paula went to make coffee. Why did Nellie forget about her daughter so often? She knew it was her mother-in-law's condition, but it hurt her to keep repeating the same things over and over again. Never mind, she told herself yet again. At least Sophie wanted to come home to see them. If Bella didn't want to, it was no skin off her nose. Perhaps she might come to a family gathering, though she doubted it.

⋆ ⋆ ⋆

Soon it was Friday, the day Sophie was coming back. Paula felt excited at the thought of a good long gossip with her daughter. If William could be persuaded to stay in with his mother, she planned to take her out to do some shopping and have a coffee. There was a new coffee shop she really wanted to try, and this would make the perfect excuse.

'I want to take Sophie out on Saturday morning. Will you stay in with your mother?' she asked her husband.

'Oh, I was planning to go to the golf club,' William replied. 'Usually a good crowd there on Saturdays. Sorry.'

'Oh William, please stay in with her. I don't see all that much of our daughter, and this seems an ideal opportunity for some mother-and-daughter time.'

'Sorry, love. I've sort of arranged it now.'

'Can't you go on Sunday instead?'

'Not really. Jack and Thomas won't

be there on Sunday.'

'I think it's incredibly selfish of you,' Paula said curtly. 'I don't ask you to do much for your mother. I'm with her most days while you do your own thing.' Suddenly she lost her temper. 'Well, you can jolly well get someone to come in and look after her. I'm going out.' She stormed into the kitchen and left him standing open-mouthed in the hall.

'Paula, wait.' When she didn't come back, he gave a shrug. If that was the way she wanted it, so be it. He was not going to give up his Saturday-morning golf, and felt sure she wouldn't leave Nellie on her own. She and Sophie could both enjoy themselves at home.

At seven-thirty Paula went off to the station to collect her daughter. William saw her going and said nothing. He assumed dinner was left ready in the oven and went into his study, where he sat down with the paper.

Nellie was sitting in the lounge, waiting for someone to call her for dinner. When nothing happened, she rose and went into the kitchen. Where on earth had everyone gone? She looked in the little sitting room where the housekeeper had always been, and still there was nobody there. She opened the back door and looked outside, but there was no one around. It was quite chilly outside and beginning to get dark.

She wandered down the street and looked around, not really recognising anything. Turning into another street, she remembered where she was, and turned towards the park. She remembered the park, where she used to take William when he was younger. She felt weary and looked for somewhere to sit down, deciding on the wall near the gates. They were closed now and seemed to be locked. It wasn't supposed to be like that. She stayed there, getting very cold.

★　★　★

Paula came back with Sophie rather later than expected. 'Hello,' she called when she was inside the house. It was very quiet everywhere; the house seemed to be deserted. 'Where is everyone?' she asked.

'I don't know,' Sophie replied. 'Perhaps they've gone out somewhere, night-clubbing or something. Dad's probably taken Grandma to the latest local hot spot. Oh, it's good to be home.'

'I'll just put the vegetables on and see where your father is.'

'Maybe he's sitting with Grandma in the lounge. I'll go if you like.' She ran upstairs and looked in the lounge. Nobody was there. 'Dad,' she called, 'where are you?' She went along to look in his study and found him fast asleep in his chair. 'Wakey, wakey,' she called to him. 'It's me, home again.'

'Oh, Sophie. Lovely to see you, darling. How are you?' He rose and gave her a hug.

'Fine, thanks. So where's Grandma?'

'I'm not sure. In the lounge, probably.'

41

'No she isn't. I went there first to look for you.'

'Perhaps she's in her room. I'll go and look. You go on down. I'll come and get us a drink when I've found her.'

'Okay, Dad. I'll go and see if Mum needs any help.' She ran down the stairs and went into the kitchen. 'Guess what? Dad was fast asleep in his study. I suspect he was reading the newspaper and dozed off.'

'Really? And where's Grandma?'

'Don't know. Dad thinks she may be in her room. What's for dinner?'

'I've made a pie. It's keeping warm in the oven. Just waiting for the carrots to cook. Won't be more than a moment or two.'

'Great. Nothing like your pies. Where are we eating?'

'In the dining room. Nellie likes to eat in there. Mind you, I get sick of being called the cook all the time. She's deteriorated quite a bit recently. Keeps forgetting things and asking the same thing over and over. I'm not sure what will happen. Thought I'd better warn you. The doctor suggested an infection, but she's not showing any signs of improvement. Right, these are done. I'll get the vegetable dish out.'

William came into the room looking distraught. 'Mum's disappeared,' he announced. 'She isn't anywhere in the house. I've looked everywhere I can think of.'

'Didn't you sit with her when I went to collect Sophie?' Paula asked him.

'Didn't think. I assumed she'd be all right.'

'Oh good heavens. Where on earth has she gone? Really, William, you know she can't be left on her own for long.'

'I didn't know she was in such a bad way.'

'I've been telling you for long enough that she can't be left alone. Perhaps she's gone out. Oh dear, and dinner is ready now. I'll have to leave it in the oven and go and look for her. I'm so sorry to greet your weekend home like this, Sophie. It's all down to your father,' she added crossly.

'I'll put my coat on and look round the garden,' Sophie offered. 'Perhaps she's outside looking at the plants.'

'Thanks, love,' Paula said gratefully. 'I'll go along the street and see if she's there.'

'Where shall I look?' asked William helplessly.

'Further afield, I should think,' Paula told him. 'We've no idea how long she's been out. Could be ever since I left for the station. She could have gone a long way in that time.'

'Shall I take the car?' he asked.

'If you like. She'll probably be tired if she's walked a long way and will be glad of a lift home again.'

'Right you are. I'll drive round the local streets and hope I can spot her.' He seemed happier with something to do, possibly because it helped salve his guilt. He drove off at a rate of knots and Paula sighed. He'd never even see Nellie if he went at that speed.

She gave a shrug and went along

their own road. On the way she saw a couple of folks walking and asked them if they'd seen Nellie, but they shook their heads and apologised. She turned at the end of their road and looked along the next street, but there was still no sign of her mother-in-law, so she went back home again and met Sophie.

'No luck?' Paula asked as she came in.

'No sign of her anywhere in the garden,' Sophie replied. 'And nor along the street, I gather?'

'Why on earth did she have to go off tonight, of all nights? I was so hoping to have a nice peaceful evening chatting and relaxing. Do you think I ought to phone the police?'

'I'm not sure. It depends on where she's actually gone. How bad is she now?'

'Pretty confused. Unfortunately, the doctor hasn't offered any real help. She could go on like this forever. I'm not sure who'd pop their clogs first.'

'Oh Mum, don't talk like that.'

'It does seem so sad, though, when you think how she used to be,' Paula sighed. 'So dynamic and organised. I think she started to go downhill when the company was sold. Seemed to lose her motivation. She doesn't realise it's gone. Still asks how it's going, and wants to go in and take a look round.'

'Goodness, I didn't know it was like that. I must tell Bella. It really is time she came home, isn't it?'

'I know Nellie would like to see her.'

'Perhaps I might ring her. Not that she'll be in during the evening. Perhaps I can ring in the morning. Who knows, maybe she'll even come tomorrow.'

'See how it goes with what's left of the rest of this evening. I was hoping to take you out tomorrow, but it means your father would be baby-sitting her. He says he's made arrangements to play golf. Typical. He's always out somewhere.'

'That doesn't sound fair. He should do his share of looking after Nellie. Sorry, I mean Grandma.'

'Yes, well, perhaps if you tell him. I'd better check on dinner. It'll all be burnt if I leave it in the oven much longer.'

'I think I heard the car. I'll go and look.' Sophie rushed to the front door and saw the car pulling into the drive. 'He's found her,' she called back. She went outside to open the door and welcome them back. 'Hello, Grandma. Wherever have you been?'

'Bella? Is that you, dear? I am so glad to see you.'

'It's Sophie, Grandma. Come on in. Where did you find her, Dad?'

'Sitting outside the park. She's rather cold, so let's get her inside quickly.'

Sophie led her inside, calling out to her mother. Then she took her grandmother into the lounge and sat her close to the fire.

'There you are. You'll soon be warm again. I'll go and tell Mum.' She ran to the kitchen, where her mother was berating her father. 'Hey there,' Sophie said, 'she's okay now.'

'It really is irresponsible of you,

William,' Paula said, ignoring Sophie and looking daggers at him. 'Not a lot to ask, to look after your own mother for five minutes, surely. Let's go and see if the food is still edible. I'll take it into the dining room, and William, you can take your mother there.'

'I'll help, Mum,' offered Sophie. She carried one of the dishes through to the dining room and put it on the table. She smiled at the table, beautifully set out and with the best cloth. Was it just for her benefit, or was this the usual way her mother did things? Possibly the latter. Nellie seemed to expect everything to go on the way it always had done, despite the fact that they no longer had staff to help. She knew how much her mother tried to keep things going and how difficult it often was. Her mother came in with the rest of the meal.

'Where's your father?' Paula asked.

'Collecting Grandma, I assume.'

'Go and give him a shout, will you? I refuse to ring the gong, though Nellie would probably like me to.'

Sophie went into the hall and called out that dinner was on the table. 'Dad? Ready,' she shouted again, more loudly.

'All right, all right. No need to sound like a screaming banshee. We're on our way. Come along, Mother. Dinner's on the table.'

'I didn't hear the gong, did you? And does your father know it's ready?'

'Come on, Mother, before it gets cold.'

'Is anyone else coming this evening?' she asked William as she sat down.

'Just us tonight, with Paula and Sophie here,' he answered.

'Now, would you like some pie?' Paula offered. 'Goodness, I hope it's still edible,' she added, cutting into the somewhat overcooked pastry.

'I'm sure it'll be lovely. I'm starving after the adventure,' Sophie told them.

'Oh, you've been having adventures, have you, dear? Do tell us all about them. I'm sure Paula would like to hear some cheerful stories, wouldn't you, dear?'

'It's all right, Nellie, I know all about them,' Paula said. 'Now, some carrots? I'm sure William will help you.'

'I don't like carrots. Get me something else.'

'There isn't anything else. You ate them yesterday, so get on with them now.' Paula was irritated beyond measure. 'Sophie, there's yours.'

'Thanks, Mum. Looks lovely.'

Paula smiled at her daughter. At least someone was grateful. She was determined to take Sophie out the next day, even if it did mean her husband would have to stay in and miss his wretched golf.

The rest of the evening passed reasonably smoothly, and Nellie went off to bed about ten o'clock. William also drifted off to his study and left the two women on their own. Sophie poured out her concerns regarding Bella.

'Very difficult to think of her as my aunt. I always think aunts should be much older — and Bella, well she seems younger than I am.'

'You don't think it's working out, then?'

'Not really. I'd much rather live on my own than with her, but there's nothing I can do about that.'

'You could get a place of your own. Move out.'

'That's all very well, but I can't exactly afford anything else.'

'I could help you out. Mum left me some money. I could buy somewhere for you to live. You could always pay me rent if it worries you. Not a big rent, of course. Minimum amount or nothing, if you'd accept it.'

'That's very generous of you.'

'Well, think about it. It may be the answer to your problems.'

'Sounds marvellous. I'd only have to cook for myself, and I could do my own shopping without thinking of what Bella wants all the time. She's a terror for using things in the flat without asking. I bought some shampoo last week and she'd used half of it before I'd even tried it.'

'Think about it, anyway. The offer's there.'

'I certainly will. Thank you, Mum.'

They chatted for a while longer until Paula was almost falling asleep. 'Must go to bed,' she said. 'We'll definitely go out tomorrow. There's a new shopping centre in Hanley. We'll have coffee and it will be a lovely morning.'

'Thanks, Mum. For everything. I'll give Bella a call tomorrow before we go out and tell her she needs to come home to see her mum before it's too late.'

Paula thought about what her daughter had said as she was getting into bed. Surely she didn't think Nellie was getting close to the end of her life? She hadn't really thought about it herself; had assumed there would be some sort of cure offered before too long. If Nellie deteriorated much more, could Paula possibly cope? Goodness, she thought, it was bad enough now. If Nellie got much worse, they'd have to get someone in to look after her.

Paula lay awake for some time, thinking over the possibilities. It certainly would be a relief to have someone else in the house to help with her mother-in-law. She made up her mind to tackle William with her ideas the next day. Maybe it would be easier to convince him if she left him alone with his mother for the morning.

4

Bella was shocked when she discovered Sophie had gone away. She cursed her for leaving on a Friday before she'd even done the shopping, and realised she'd have to go on her own if she were to eat over the weekend. Setting this thought aside for now, she phoned one of her friends and went out for the evening, and came back rather late, determined to have a good lie-in the next morning. The best-laid plans and all that, she realised when the phone was ringing at nine o'clock.

'Hallo? I hope you know what time it is,' she greeted her caller.

'Bella, it's Sophie. I'm at home with Mum and Dad.'

'You might have told me you were going to be away.'

'I did. I told you yesterday morning.'

'Oh, did you? I must have missed

that. What do you want?'

'I think you should come home and see your mother. She's really gone downhill. She wants to see you, too. You could catch the train this morning and be here by lunchtime.'

'I'm sorry, but I have plans.'

'You really are the most selfish person I know. I'm telling you this because your mother is ill. She's got something like dementia and is in a dreadful state.'

'How ill? I mean, is she going to die?'

'I don't know. But she wants to see you. I really think you should come.'

'I'll think about it. Let me talk to Paula. She'll be a bit more practical than you.'

'She's busy,' Sophie replied crossly, 'looking after your mother.'

'I'm sure she can cope. She always does. Enjoy your weekend. See you when you get back.'

Bella put the phone down and sat back in her chair. Now she was awake, she thought she might make some breakfast and stay up. She looked in the breadbin, but there was no bread, nor was there any cereal. It was rotten of Sophie to go away and leave her without anything to eat. It never even occurred to Bella to do any shopping, and she simply cursed her flatmate. Perhaps she should go out for breakfast . . . or perhaps she should go and see her mother.

If only she had a car. It would be so much easier than travelling by train. Perhaps Tom would take her — but then, she had been out with him twice this week, and thought she might be wearing his friendship rather thin. No, it would have to be the train or nothing. That seemed like quite a lot of effort for her, so she decided to go into town and get some breakfast. There were definitely places that did all-day breakfasts. Feeling much more enthusiastic, she dressed and set off for town.

Bella was never a person to be inconvenienced; and, having waited a few minutes for a bus, she hailed a passing taxi.

'City centre, please. As fast as you like.'

'Certainly, madam. Anywhere in particular?'

'Clock tower, I should think.'

She watched the city passing by the window and thought again about getting a car. A small car would make so much difference to her life. Perhaps if she had gone home, she could have persuaded her mother to buy one for her.

'Changed my mind,' she said to the driver. 'Drop me at the station, please.'

'Right you are. Station it is.' He swung round at the next junction and did as instructed.

Bella paid him, hoping she had enough left for her ticket and breakfast. She felt extremely hungry and was ready to eat a huge meal. Perhaps she could use her credit card to pay for her ticket. It was almost up to the hilt, but she felt sure it would be all right.

The ticket collector stared at her as she booked and handed over her card. 'This is almost up to its limit,' he told her.

'Still valid, though, isn't it?'

'Well, okay, I'll let it through this time. Stoke-on-Trent, did you say?'

She nodded. He handed her the bill to sign and she smiled as she took the ticket. It was only a single, but she knew her mother would always give her a handout. She went into the station buffet and ordered a full English breakfast; there was half an hour to wait, which would be plenty of time. She really should phone and get someone to collect her from the station, but she decided she'd get a taxi and get her mother to pay for it when she arrived. She settled down to enjoy her breakfast.

★ ★ ★

Once Bella arrived at Stoke station, she looked for a taxi. She had to wait for several minutes, and cursed slightly, but then one arrived and she leapt into it.

'Cobridge House, Longton,' she snapped to the driver.

'Where's that?' he asked.

'Oh for heaven's sake. Don't you even know the area? It's near the park, about a mile outside the town.'

'Very well, madam. Perhaps you can direct me further when we're closer.'

She didn't reply, but sat back and waited until they were closer to her one-time home. She could see a few changes in the area: new houses and some large estates to one side, and then a few different shops to satisfy the new customers. Perhaps Stoke and its surroundings were waking up after all.

'Turn right up the next road and continue straight on. Then it's a left turn at the top.' She spoke in her usual bored way of addressing lesser mortals. When they got to her road, she told him to pull into the drive and then wait for a few minutes while she went inside to collect his fare.

'You mean to say you don't have enough money?' he said, spluttering slightly.

'Oh, they'll soon give me some money. Don't fret, dear, you'll get paid.'

She ran to the door and pushed at it, then rang the bell continually. At last William came to answer it, looking rather grumpy.

'Bella. What on earth are you doing here?'

'Give me some money for my taxi. Come on, the meter's ticking away.'

'How much do you need?'

'Oh I don't know. A fiver should do it.'

'You really are the limit. Wait there; I'll have to go and find some money.'

The driver got out and stood there, looking menacing.

'Keep your hair on,' Bella told him. 'My brother's gone to get your money.'

William came back with some cash and handed it to the taxi driver.

'Thanks very much, sir. Have a nice day.' He drove away and left Bella watching him.

'Ignorant slob,' Bella muttered. 'So how's Mum?' she asked her brother, going inside and hanging her coat up. 'I gather she's very unwell, according to

Sophie. Where is she, by the way?'

'Sophie and Paula have gone shopping. I've missed my golf this morning and have been sitting with Mum, feeling nauseatingly bored. Now you're here, perhaps you can organise something for us to eat.'

'Me? You're joking, of course. When will the others be back? Can't they do it?'

'Come on, Bella. You can make a sandwich, surely?'

'I've come to see Mother. Where is she?'

'In the lounge. I've got the radio on in hopes that it will interest her.'

'I'll go and face her, then. I mean, she won't attack me or anything, will she?'

'Attack you? Where on earth have you got that idea?'

'I'm hoping she's going to cough up some cash for me. I've spent all mine on the train fare.'

'Don't even think of asking her. She doesn't have any cash.'

'What do you mean? She's loaded. Or have you taken all of it for yourself?'

'Don't be stupid. Most of the cash is invested in this house, and your flat didn't come cheap either. We manage on a relatively small amount each month. The days of affluence are long gone.'

Bella stared at him, clearly not believing what she was hearing. Her family were extremely wealthy, everyone knew that, and she was only working for pocket money.

'But you sold the factory and the business. It must have been well worth doing.'

'The money we got from that has been invested. You got your share with us buying your flat. Paula does pretty much all the work around here. We have a woman who comes in to clean, but the cooking and looking after our mother, well, that's down to my wife.'

'But I need a car. I need Mother to buy it for me.'

'What on earth do you need a car for?'

'To come here, for one thing. I don't suppose you've ever had to put up with trains. It takes an age, and, well, it's very uncomfortable sitting with all the other people. I may have to go back first class.'

'Depends if you can afford it, doesn't it?'

'I'm going to see Mum now,' Bella told him, totally ignoring what he'd said. While she opened the door of the lounge and peered round it, William disappeared into the kitchen. She was shocked at the sight of her mother sitting there almost asleep and with her mouth open.

'Mummy? Hallo. It's me, Bella.'

'Bella?' Nellie said. 'Oh my goodness me. Bella. How wonderful to see you. Have you ordered tea? Come and give me a kiss.'

Bella went over to her mother and allowed her lips to brush casually against the offered cheek. Nellie's hands reached out to grab her but she managed to shrug her away.

'How are you feeling?' Bella asked.

'Very well. They don't let me work anymore, you know. I wanted to go into the factory but they just keep me at home. I've got so many ideas for new designs.'

'Perhaps you can draw them out here? Make your plans on paper and give them to William to follow up?'

'That's a very good idea. Can you find me some paper to draw on?'

'Of course I will.'

'I'm feeling very hungry. Is Cook preparing luncheon? Now you're here, we can eat in the dining room. It'll make a change from the kitchen.'

'You mean you usually eat in the kitchen?' Bella said in horror.

'Oh yes, dear. Just a snack, you know. I don't much like the sort of snacks we have these days.'

'And what sort of snacks do you have?' Bella was growing increasingly worried by her mother's remarks. Surely they weren't starving her?

'Oh, I don't know. Anything lying around, it seems to me. Can't you make me something tasty, like I used to have? Your father would never put up with all this economising. We always used to have good meals. Two cooked meals every day. Now it's just a sandwich.'

Bella thought back to William's comment when she arrived. *Surely you can make a sandwich*. It seemed a good job she'd come when she had. Clearly, she should have come a lot sooner.

'I'll go and see what I can find,' Bella told her mother. 'Don't worry, I'll soon make something nice for you.'

She went into the kitchen, where her brother was standing and looking helpless. He had a loaf on the table and a packet of ham. 'What are you doing?' she challenged him.

'I was thinking of making some sandwiches. There's ham to use. I'll leave it to you if you're here.'

'Sandwiches? Is that the best you can do?'

'We usually have sandwiches for lunch. Paula usually does them but she seems to have forgotten today. I suppose she's enjoying herself with Sophie. I expect they're having lunch in town somewhere. No thought for us.'

'I think Mum is expecting something a bit better than sandwiches. She was saying she and Dad always had two cooked meals every day. Have your standards slipped so far down?'

'Maybe they have. But I can't expect Paula to cook twice in a day.'

'This really isn't good enough. You need to get a proper cook. Even I manage to eat properly each day. Sophie usually does the evening meal, and I eat in the canteen or at one of our local cafés. I'd better look in the fridge and see what I can find.'

She looked and saw some chops. 'Good. I suppose I can manage to grill these. Do you want two?' He nodded. 'What about Mum? Will she eat two?'

'I expect so. What will you make with them?'

'Perhaps some salad and bread. It'll be quicker.'

'Jolly good. I'll leave you to it, then.

I'd better go back to Mother, or she'll go wandering off somewhere again.'

'Wandering off? What does that mean?'

'She went last night. No idea where she was going, but I drove out to find her. She was up near the park. Frozen nearly solid.'

'Good heavens. She needs a nurse to look after her, William. You must get things organised. Get a cook and get a nurse. There's plenty of room here for them. Open up the old servants' quarters and let them live in.' While she was talking, she was organising the chops on the grill pan. She put it on to heat and found some tired lettuce leaves and tomatoes.

'We are actually thinking of moving to somewhere smaller,' William explained. 'Paula wants less work and a more modern place. Trouble is, Nellie won't even contemplate it. This place will fetch quite a decent price. We've actually had someone come round wanting it for flats.'

'How ghastly.'

'It may seem ghastly, but it could be profitable.'

'Maybe. I could have my car then, couldn't I?'

'You'll be lucky. As I said, you've had your share in the form of the flat. Are those chops all right? Looks as if they're cooking rather too fast.'

'Damnation. Oh well, you can cut off the burnt bits. I told you I was useless at cooking.'

'I'll go and see Mother,' William announced, retreating quickly from the room.

Bella plonked some salad onto three plates and put bread on another. The chops were cooking better now she'd turned the heat down, and soon they were ready. Should she lay the table in the dining room? Perhaps it would make her mother happier if she did. She went found a tablecloth, then took out the best silver and laid three places.

'Ready,' she called. 'Take Mum into the dining room, William, and I'll bring the meal in.' She put it all onto a tray and carried it in.

'How nice,' said Nellie. 'Just like the old days. Isn't your father coming to join us?'

'What?' Bella exclaimed.

'Your father, dear. I assumed he was still in the house.'

Bella stared at her brother, desperately hoping he'd say something. When he didn't, she said, 'Father isn't here anymore.'

'Don't start that all over again,' Nellie chided her. 'I told you, I was talking to him only half an hour ago.'

'Here you are, Mum,' Bella said, ignoring the remark as she gave Nellie a plate of food. 'Can you manage to cut it yourself?'

'Of course I can. I'm not senile, you know. Honestly, you youngsters have no faith in us older folks.'

They all ate almost in silence. The chops weren't too bad, considering, Bella thought.

'Thanks for cooking the lunch,' William said. 'Made a change.'

'Good. Did you enjoy it, Mum?' Bella asked her.

'Bit tough. Never mind. I did enjoy having a proper meal.'

'I'll clear away then,' Bella said, getting up.

'What's for dessert?' Nellie asked.

'Oh. I haven't made anything. Would you like some fruit?'

'I want a proper pudding.'

'Well, I'm sorry, but I haven't had time to make anything.'

'Not good enough. I want a proper pudding.'

Bella looked helplessly at William. 'What can I do?'

'You'll have to wait for supper, Mum,' he said. 'Paula will make something then.'

'But I haven't had a proper dinner. No pudding means I'll be hungry.' She moaned like a small child, and her daughter was at a loss.

Bella cleared the plates away and escaped into the kitchen, then dumped them in the sink and put the kettle on.

Perhaps if she made coffee, Nellie would forget about the lack of pudding. She made three cups and put them on the tray.

'Coffee, everyone,' she said cheerfully, wishing she actually felt cheerful. It was depressing here, and the sooner she could get away, the better.

'How lovely, Bella, dear. It's very good of you to look after us so well. Don't you think so, William?'

'Very good. I wonder when Paula and Sophie will be back. They've been gone such a long time. Does Sophie know you're here?' he asked Bella.

'She ordered me to come, so I expect so.'

'How do you mean, she ordered you?'

'Well, she phoned me this morning at some ungodly hour and said I should come home. Here I am. Then I discover she's gone out. Typical of her.'

'Who's gone out?' asked Nellie.

'Paula and Sophie,' William replied.

'Where have they gone?'

'Shopping,' he told her. 'I'm sure they'll be back soon.'

'I hope so, or they'll miss my party.'

'What party's that, Mum?' Bella asked.

'Paula's inviting all the family over. I'm having a new dress for the occasion.'

Bella looked at William for confirmation. He nodded as if to say she was quite right.

'That will be nice, won't it?' Bella said. 'How are all the family? Goodness, it's a long time since I saw some of them.'

'There's Joe and Billy and Lizzie. Is that everyone, dear?' asked Nellie.

'And all their families,' William answered. 'I don't know if they'll all come, but we can invite them at least. Amazing to think that some of their children have got children of their own.'

They spent a few minutes listing them all and came to the conclusion they wouldn't even have room for all of them. 'I think we'll have to invite just the parents,' William concluded. 'If you and Sophie come as well,' he added, addressing Bella, 'it'll make a good number.'

'Depends when it is,' Bella replied. 'I'm not sure what I'm doing.'

'Means a lot to Mum having you here. Perhaps you can try your best.'

'If I had a car, it might not be such a problem. I was going to ask if you'd consider buying me a car, Mum?'

'Of course I will, dear.'

'Mum, you know you can't,' William told her firmly.

'But if she wants one, surely she should have one?'

'I really do need a car. It's hopeless trying to get anywhere without one.'

'I think she should have a car, don't you, dear?'

'Thank you so much,' Bella said gleefully. 'I could go and look at some right now.'

'Bella, no, you can't,' William said. 'Mum doesn't have access to money.'

'I can write a cheque,' Nellie said.

'I'll get your chequebook for you,' Bella offered. 'Where is it?'

'She doesn't have a chequebook anymore,' William told her, beginning to sound exasperated. 'We had to take it away when she kept writing cheques to all manner of people. I'm sorry, Bella, but there isn't any money spare for you to go and buy a car. Besides, you could hardly afford to run it, could you?'

'If you gave me a fuel allowance each month, I could. Least you could do.'

'When will you get it into your head — we are running short of cash. You talk about us getting help in the home and someone to help look after Mum, but we can't afford it. Unless we sell this place and move to somewhere sensible, we shall run out of cash by . . . well, I don't know when exactly, but soon.'

'I think you're simply being selfish,' Bella said petulantly. 'But then, you always were mean-spirited.'

'I'm going to my study. I can't cope with any more of this talk. You stay with Mother till Paula gets back.' William rose and stormed out of the room.

'I'll just take the cups to the kitchen,' Bella said to her mother. 'You'll be all right for a few minutes, won't you?'

'Of course I will. I don't need someone with me all the time. I might go to my room and have a lie down. I feel quite exhausted.'

'Good. You do that.'

Bella heard the front door open, and Sophie and Paula entered the house.

'Oh, you came,' said Sophie. 'Thank goodness for that.'

5

Paula followed her daughter in and greeted Bella. 'How nice to see you. I expect your mother was pleased to see you, too.'

'I suppose she was. She's in a bit of state, isn't she?'

'Well, she's certainly suffering from something or other, but she seems happy enough. What makes you say that, anyway?' Paula was puzzled by Bella's remarks.

'I disagree. I find her disturbed and feeling rather sad. Nothing is the same anymore. Talking to my brother, I begin to see why. She's feeling deprived of something to do. Her midday meal has been withdrawn, and she never eats in the dining room anymore. She needs someone to look after her properly. If you're finding the cooking too much to cope with, you need a proper full-time cook.'

'I see. And have you said all this to your brother?'

'I certainly have.'

'And what did he say?'

'Some baloney about you not having money. I've never heard anything like it. Everyone knows you made a fortune selling the company. He says it's all invested and can't be touched. I want a car, and Mother says she'd like to buy me one, but he won't let her even have a chequebook.'

'Well, I'm sorry to hear that,' Paula said curtly. 'I'm also sorry you don't seem to have any idea about the money we got for the factory. A certain amount was invested for the future, but we bought a flat for you two to live in. Remember that? I know it wasn't a huge thing in your estimation, but it was over half the money we got. It was hardly a vast amount of money we received from the sale, as the business was failing. We were lucky to get as much as we did.

'As for employing people to work

here, well, we decided we could pay one cleaning woman to come in for a couple of hours, and I'd do the rest. Oh, and as for Nellie never eating in the dining room, we eat there every night. And she does have lunch every day. Not a cooked meal most days, but she does eat very well.' Paula was angry and had let herself speak out.

'Well, at least she's eaten properly today,' Bella said. 'I cooked some chops I found in the fridge. She ate the lot.'

'Oh, well done. They were for supper. I suppose I'd better go and buy something else, assuming you're stay-ing?'

'I'll go back after lunch tomorrow. What time are you going, Sophie?'

'I was planning to leave after tea. We could travel together if you like. Perhaps Mum can give us a lift to the station?'

'Of course I will. How did you get from the station, Bella?'

'Taxi, of course.'

'Wow. Get you. How much did that

cost?' asked Sophie.

'William paid.'

'That was nice of him,' Paula said. 'I'd better get to the butcher's before he closes. I've got a beef joint for tomorrow. I think there'll be enough. Do you want to put the kettle on and make some tea, Sophie? I'd kill for a cuppa. You can make it ready for my return.' She went off again and the two girls looked at each other.

'You really are the limit, Bella,' Sophie sighed. 'Still, at least you proved you could cook something.'

'I burned it. Had to cut it all away. I'm useless in the kitchen. I'll go and sit in the lounge. Bring my tea in there, will you? And if you find any cake, I can always manage a slice or two.'

'I hope you're looking after Grandma.'

'She's gone to her room for a rest. Peace everywhere.'

Sophie went into the kitchen and saw the dirty dishes. 'Oh honestly, Bella!' She stomped off to the lounge and almost yelled at her aunt. 'Come and wash up your dirty lunch dishes. You are so lazy — how can you just leave them there for Mum to sort out?'

'Sorry, love. I don't want to mess up my nails, and I don't have a change of clothes with me.'

'So what? There's always a pinny on the side. And some rubber gloves. Nobody else is going to do your dirty washing-up.'

'I bet Paula will do it. She's been gadding about all day. So have you, come to think of it. You can do it between you. Where did you go, by the way?'

'Up to Hanley. There's a new shopping centre there. Had some lunch in a new coffee bar.'

'Well, bully for you. Buy anything nice?'

'Not a lot. I got some fabric I liked from the market.'

'Not more sewing, surely? By the way, I meant to ask you — what was with the evening dress?'

'What evening dress?' Sophie asked,

knowing exactly what Bella meant.

'The one you sent to be made. I believe you let Mr Hill think it was my design?'

'Oh. Yes.' She paused. 'You were away that day, so I did it anyway.'

'Not my style at all.'

'No, but he liked it. I liked it too.'

'Oh well, too late now. It's already well on its way. I just hope it sells. I may have to admit to it being yours if it doesn't.'

'That sounds about typical of you. You'd better get into the kitchen and do your washing-up.'

'Can't you do it for me? I do feel pretty exhausted.'

'No, I will not. And don't you dare leave it for Mum to do. She won't be pleased.'

'Oh all right, after I've had some tea.'

'No, you do it now, before Mum gets back.'

'Oh honestly. All right, slave driver. What did your last slave die of?' Grumbling all the way, Bella followed

Sophie into the kitchen. She pulled on some rubber gloves and tied an apron round her middle, then ran hot water over all the plates and practically emptied the tank. Sophie watched her working and said nothing, then made a pot of tea and took out some cups and saucers.

'I'll have a mug, thank you,' said Bella.

'I'm not sure there are any mugs. You'll have to have a cup, same as everyone else. What about Grandma — will she want any?'

'Doubt it. She went to bed for the afternoon, so we probably won't see her till dinnertime. There, that's that lot done.'

'You'll need to dry them. There's a tea towel on the rack.'

'They can drip dry. I'm ready for my tea now. Is there any cake?'

'No idea.'

Bella started opening tins and eventually found a Victoria sponge. She cut herself a large slice and put the lid back on the tin. Sophie watched her and shook her head. She really was the most selfish woman she had ever met. She expected her mother had been saving the cake for tea tomorrow, and now it was spoiled.

'That's good,' Bella said. 'Think I'll have some more.' She opened the tin again and cut herself a second large slice. Sophie watched her and said nothing. She felt very helpless, and poured her tea and took a cup for her father. She couldn't bear to watch her aunt. Feeling somewhat cowardly, she decided she would have a word with William about her.

He was sitting reading the newspaper up in his study. Sophie tapped on the door and went in. 'Brought you a cup of tea.'

'Thank you, dear. Very good of you. How are you getting on?'

'Me? I'm ready to murder your sister. She's a total pain. And so greedy. Sorry, I'm just so annoyed with her.'

'What's she done now?'

'She'd left your washing up in the sink, for a start. I persuaded her to see to it, but she won't dry it. Then she decided she wanted some cake and she's eaten a mass of it. I bet Mum had made it for tea tomorrow. Oh honestly, Dad, she's driving me mad. Mum's suggested I find somewhere else to live if I really can't cope.'

'How will you afford it?'

She stared at her father. 'I don't know yet. Early stages. Meanwhile, I have to do all the cooking and shopping, and Bella just comes and goes as she pleases.'

'But she pays her way, doesn't she?' Sophie shook her head. 'You mean you pay for all the food and other shopping?'

'Well, yes.'

'But that's not fair at all. She pays her share of the electricity and gas, surely?'

'More or less. I usually pay for the phone — which again isn't really fair, as she uses it more than I do.'

'I can see she needs a jolly good

talking to. She must have plenty of savings.'

'Not really. Her credit card is up to its limit. I saw her bill for last month.'

'I'll have a talk with her. Where is she?'

'Scoffing cake the last time I saw her, in the kitchen.'

'Thanks for the tea. I'll go and see her now. You relax a bit. And don't worry, I'll sort her out one way or another.'

'Thanks, Dad. I'll stay out of your way for a while. Guess I'll see how Grandma is.'

William went downstairs and looked for his sister. She wasn't in the kitchen, but the tin with the cake in it had been left on the table, the lid off. He went into the lounge and found Bella sitting on the sofa, her feet up and her shoes still on.

'Ah, Bella. I need to talk to you.'

'Oh don't start. I expect Sophie's been moaning about me, hasn't she?'

'Well, yes. With good cause.'

'So what have I done now to displease her ladyship?'

He told her in no uncertain terms about everything from not doing her share of the work to not helping with the bills.

'I can't help it. She doesn't have to spend money like I do.'

'But you earn more than Sophie does, don't you?'

'So what? Just because she stays in most nights and does her wretched sewing, doesn't mean I can't go out and have a life. She'll die an old maid with no experience of living.'

'At least she'll make someone a good wife. She can cook and manage a house far better than you can.'

'Well good for her. She'll never meet anyone, though, will she? I have a string of men after me. Always have a choice of who to go out with and where to go.'

'While Sophie stays at home doing the cooking and cleaning.'

'She doesn't have to. If she chooses to do it, that's up to her.'

'And if she doesn't?'

'Then it gets left till she does. Now, have you finished? You're totally boring me.'

'Tough. I want you to give her a fair share of money to do the shopping. If she's going to continue to do it, she needs you to pay.'

'If I had it, I'd give it to her willingly. But I don't. In fact, if Mother won't give me any to buy a car, I shall expect you to hand it out. Nothing too expensive; a couple of thousand should do it. You both have cars, so it's only fair. And I'll need about two hundred a year for running costs.'

'When you can afford to buy it for yourself, you can have it. You really are the limit, Bella. I think if Sophie wants to move out, it might be a good idea.'

'Move out? Don't be ridiculous. How could she afford it?'

'I don't know. Perhaps if she only had herself to look after, that would make a difference. I'm going to see if Paula's back. Think about it. Either you pay your way, or she'll find somewhere else to live.'

Bella sat back and laughed. How on earth could the girl live anywhere else? Sophie was, of course, exaggerating the amount of work she had to do. And if she were shopping for her own food, she might just as well buy enough for Bella too. Sophie was mostly in the flat anyway, so she might as well do the cleaning. As for Bella, she couldn't care less whether the place was pristine or not.

★   ★   ★

Paula was back and clearing the kitchen, while William stood drinking a cup of tea. The lunch dishes she had dried and put away. The cake in the tin was still on the table. 'I see you all had some of tomorrow's cake,' she said grumpily.

'No, we didn't,' William said. 'It was all Bella's doing. She found it and decided to eat it.'

'Oh, really? How utterly piggish of her. I should have hidden it away somewhere. And Sophie had a moan about her while we were out; that's why we were so long. She simply poured it all out.'

'She did the same to me. I've had a talk to Bella, but I doubt it did any good. I think Sophie would very much like to move out of their flat, actually.'

'I've told her I'll help her.'

'You will? How?'

'I've still got the money my mother left me. I can use that.'

'That's very generous of you,' William said. 'I thought you were saving that for a rainy day.'

'Yes, well I think the rain is pouring down at present.'

'So what's going to happen now?'

'Sophie's going to look around and see what she can find. I've given her my limit and so we shall see. I don't want to discuss it in front of Bella for a while, so keep it to yourself.'

'Okay. As you like, dear.'

Paula put her hands on her hips and

looked thoughtful. 'I suppose I'd better start on dinner next. I've bought a chicken to roast. Hope that's all right.'

'I'm sure it'll be fine.'

'Pretty well all the butcher had left at this late stage of the day,' she said, getting it out of the fridge. 'I suppose there wouldn't have been enough chops anyway, with Bella here. If she'd told us she was coming . . . ah well. She came and it has cheered Nellie a bit. Where is she, by the way?'

'Nellie? I think she went to her room. Shall I go and see if she's all right?'

'You'd better. How long has she been there?'

'She went up soon after we'd finished coffee.'

'Heavens. She'll never sleep tonight if she's been asleep all this time.'

'I'll go and see if she's awake.' He ran upstairs to his mother's room and tapped on the door.

'Is it morning?' he heard her call.

'It's time you were coming downstairs,' he replied.

'Why am I wearing my day clothes?'

'You went for a rest after lunch. You must have fallen asleep.'

'Oh dear, and just when Bella's come to see me. She must think I'm terrible.'

'I don't think so at all. Come on, now. She's in the lounge, waiting for you.'

The two of them went down, and Nellie greeted Bella like a long-lost relative, which in a way she really was. She chatted to her daughter and sounded remarkably normal. William left them to it and went back to the kitchen. He sat on a stool and spoke to his wife.

'They seem okay. Sophie not down yet?'

'I think she's looking at her new fabric. Oh, apparently she's rather keen on someone at work. He's taken her for a drink on a couple of occasions. Don't say anything to her, but she sounded quite smitten.'

'That's good. According to Bella, she'll never meet anyone and will be an old maid for life.'

'Hopefully not. Perhaps she'll see more of him and won't need to move out. Wouldn't it be wonderful to see her married and settled down?'

'Now then, Paula, don't get carried away. I'm going back to my study now. Perhaps our daughter will come and keep you company. I don't want you to feel lonely.'

'It's all a case of cooking, I suppose. I know Nellie doesn't like to eat too late, and she was pushed a bit last night. Mind you, that was her own fault.'

William left her sorting out the chicken, and called out to his daughter as he went past the bedroom. Sophie went down and joined her mother in the kitchen, peeling potatoes and generally chatting.

'So what's the man's name?' Paula asked.

'Fred. I know it sounds rather boring, but that's it. Don't go getting ideas. I've only been out with him a couple of times. Well, a few times, actually.'

'And what does he do?'

'He works in sales. Very much an office job. I don't actually meet many men, unlike Bella, who seems to have a different one for each night of the week. She's welcome to them. Most of them are really boring. Don't know what she sees in them, actually, unless it's a meal ticket. Yes, I expect that's it. Don't know why they do it.'

'Some men are like that. They'll take someone out for what they can get out of it.'

'Oh. I never thought of that. She doesn't come home till very late sometimes. One day this week, she refused to come in at all. Think I told you.'

'So how's the work itself going?' Paula changed the subject.

'I love it. I'm a bit of a dogsbody for Bella, but she's very clever. Does lovely designs.'

'But so do you. I've seen them and your drawings. Don't put yourself down. Put them forward to your boss.'

'Well, actually, I did do one the other

day when Bella was away. I may have told you. I gave it to Mr Hill and he loved it. It's being made up at present. The only trouble is, he thinks Bella designed it. She didn't confess to it being mine and says she'll only let on if it's a failure.'

'Not good at all. There, I think we're done. Let's go and sit in the lounge now. It'll carry on cooking on its own.'

'Shall I make some tea then, Mum? I don't think you ever had any, did you?'

'I'll do it.'

'No, I insist you go and sit down for a bit. I'll bring it to the lounge.'

As she laid the tray, Sophie thought about her future. She loved the idea of having her own place and furnishing it to her own taste. Yes indeed, she would certainly follow her mother's advice and look for somewhere new when she got back to Leicester.

6

Bella made her appearance quite late the next day. 'What's for breakfast?' she demanded.

Paula was washing up. 'You can make some toast if you want it,' she said. 'Or there are some cornflakes. Help yourself.'

'I'd like some bacon and eggs.'

'Sorry, don't have anything like that. The kettle's recently boiled, so you can make tea or coffee.' She scowled but made herself a cup of instant coffee. 'Your mother's in the breakfast room if you want to join her.'

'I'm thinking of going back this morning,' Bella said. 'Got things to do. I'd like to get the car business settled first, though.'

'I thought it had been settled.'

'No, not at all. Mum wants me to have a car and says William controls all her money. I really need him to give me a cheque. Where is he?'

'Talking to your mother and Sophie. As I said, they're in the breakfast room. You won't get any money out of him.'

'We shall see.' She bounced off and Paula shook her head. Silly girl seemed to take in nothing she was told. Any spare money they had was for their new house, and she didn't think it was possible to prise anything out of her husband.

'Bella, darling girl. How lovely to see you,' said Nellie as Bella came into the breakfast room.

'Morning, everyone,' Bella said. 'How are you today, Mother?'

'All the better for seeing you.'

'Well, if I get my car — or should I say, *when* I get my car — I shall be able to pop over to see you much more often.'

'How lovely that would be. When do you hope to get it, dear?'

'Depends on how soon my brother comes up with the cash.'

'Can't you give it to her now, dear?' Nellie asked William.

'I don't have it to give her. In fact, I feel really sorry she can't afford to buy a car for herself. It is sad, isn't it, Mother?'

'Why on earth do you want a car, Bella?' asked Sophie. 'And why do you expect Dad to pay for it?'

'I was expecting Mum to pay for it, but he's taken away all her money and won't let her have anything to spend. That's what's sad. You'll have to give me some money for the train fare back, too. I haven't got any for that. Unless you want to drive me back, brother, dear.'

'You'll be lucky. I'm off to the golf club now. I'll see you at lunch. Unless you've left by then.'

'I might as well stay for lunch. I obviously won't get anything decent for breakfast.'

'It's after ten o'clock,' Sophie said. 'Not sure what you expected. Do you want to stay here, Grandma, or shall we go into the lounge? I'll just take the dirty things back to the kitchen. You decide where you want to be and I'll come and find you afterwards.'

'Thank you, dear. She's a good girl, isn't she?'

'Amazing,' Bella replied sarcastically.

'I think I'd like to go into the lounge. We can have a nice chat in there.'

'Okay, Mum,' Bella said. 'Not sure what we'll talk about, but the lounge it is.' She rose from the table and followed her mother into the lounge, then sat down opposite her and said, 'What do you want to talk about?'

'I don't know. Now the factory's gone, I don't have anything left to interest me.'

Bella stared at her mother. This was actually sounding quite a normal sort of conversation. Maybe she wasn't in as bad a state as the rest of them suggested. She might even ask someone, if she could think of someone to ask, about her mother's condition. Perhaps she was simply bored and not as ill as everyone thought.

'You could do some designs,' Bella said. 'There must be someone who'd like them. There are lots of factories left around the place.'

'Do you think so, dear?'

'I do, Mum. You could always try it out, anyway, couldn't you? Design some plates, for instance. You used to be good at that.'

'I might try. Can you find me some paper and pencils? And paints?'

'I'll ask William where they all went. You used to have some here.'

'Oh no, dear, not in here. I used to use a little room upstairs. It would make a mess in here.' She cast her hands around the lovely room. Bella smiled. She hadn't meant literally here in this room, with its pale blue carpet and blue and white patterned furnishings. She looked along the side at the enormous glazed cupboard with the collection of Cobridge china inside. There was one of everything the company had made over the years, including many pieces designed by Nellie herself.

'You've helped create quite a heritage, you know,' Bella observed. 'Did you do the Coronation memorabilia?'

'Most of that came from William. He used some of the approved lithographs and designed the gold edges to the plates. And the little mugs. Have you got one of them?'

'What, a Coronation mug? I used to have one once. Probably in my bedroom here. I'll have a look later. I think all the children got one, didn't we?'

'Probably.'

Bella changed the subject. 'What do you think about William and Paula's plans to move house?'

'Oh, we won't be doing that. It's just some scheme they've thought up to make me unhappy. I don't want things to change.' She was clearly getting worked up at the thought.

'We can't have you getting unhappy, now, can we? I'll go and look for some paper for you to do some drawings on.' She suddenly felt weary of listening to her mother, despite the fact that she seemed quite lucid.

'What shall I draw for you, dear?'

'Whatever comes to mind. Just sketch for a while and see what happens.'

Bella went up to William's study and looked in some of the drawers for paper and pencils — and found a heap of chequebooks, one of which was her mother's. A smile slowly spread across her face. Her mother was in good form today, and with a little help she could surely sign a cheque. Bella would fill in the details later, and then she could buy her car. No need to stint. She would make it out for a round five thousand, and that would give her a good bit extra for spending. Well, a lot extra, but she felt she deserved it.

Picking up the chequebook and a pen, she returned to the lounge. She wanted to get this sorted quickly before the rest of the family could interfere.

'I've got your chequebook here, Mum. Now you can buy me the car I wanted. You'd like it if I could come and see you more often, wouldn't you?' She knew it was a good ploy, even if she didn't actually visit more often than she did now.

'That would be nice.'

'Now, can you sign the cheque? I'll fill in the details for you later.'

'Where do I sign, dear?'

'Just here.' Bella pointed at the right place and gave Nellie the pen. The first signature wasn't very good. 'Okay, Mum, try again.' She ripped out the first cheque and gave the next one to her.

After five attempts, she decided the last one would do. 'Thank you, Mum. I'll fill the rest in now. Okay?' She picked up the book and the discarded cheques and took them back to William's study, then quickly filled in the rest of the final cheque and put the book back into the drawer. Feeling quite delighted with her efforts, she took the cheque to her room and put it safely into her bag. The rubbish cheques she also stuffed in her bag. Wouldn't do to leave them around the place. She would pay the money into her bank the next day, and by next weekend she would have her car.

When she went downstairs again, she found Sophie sitting with Nellie.

'Grandma says you went to find her some paper and pencils to do some drawing. Where are they?'

'Oh, sorry, I couldn't find any. I'm going for a walk if you're here now. Need some air.'

'I'm going to help Mum with lunch. You need to stay here. Bella — ' But she had gone. Sophie turned back to her grandmother. 'Do you want some coffee?' she asked.

'Thank you, dear. Where's Bella gone?'

'I think she's gone for a walk.'

'She said she'll come and see me more often now she's got a car.'

'I don't know what you mean, Grandma. She hasn't got a car.'

'Of course she has. I've bought her a car.'

'I'll go and make some coffee for you. I won't be long. You stay here and I'll bring it to you.' She went into the kitchen, where Paula was busy making pastry for a pie. 'I don't know what Bella's up to. Grandma seems to think she's bought her a car.'

'Oh, not that again,' Paula sighed. 'Bella's fixed on the idea of getting a car. She must have talked about it to Nellie, and now she thinks she's bought it.'

'Poor old love. She's very confused, isn't she?'

'I'm afraid so. I'm not sure how much longer we can go on like this. Everything takes so much longer to explain, and she's needing more and more help.'

'She wanted some paper and pencils to do some drawing. Do you know where there are any?'

'In your father's study, bottom drawer of his desk. She'll need a board to rest on too. I think there's one of those in the scullery. Perhaps it would be a good idea. Can you get what she needs?'

'Of course. I just came to fetch her a

cup of coffee. Bella's gone out for a walk, so I shouldn't be too long. I'll take the coffee up first and then look for the other stuff. It might keep her happy for a while.'

'Thank you, Sophie. It may work. Trouble is, she's so shaky now, I don't think she can hold the pencil still enough to actually achieve much. There, that should do. Thought I'd make an apple pie.'

'Lovely. You're like Gran. She used to make wonderful pies. I'm glad she taught you how to do it.'

'Darned good job she did. We'd starve if I couldn't cook. When I think of the staff that used to keep this place going . . . '

'Your aunt used to be the house-keeper, didn't she?' Sophie asked.

'Oh yes. Auntie Wyn was here for years, and then she went to live with Mum. I miss them both terribly.'

'I'm sorry, Mum. But they did have a few years together when they were retired.'

'Yes, I was very grateful to Wyn. She helped nurse Mum at the end, when the cancer overtook her. But you might remember that. You were quite small, but you were always a part of it.'

'I'd better take Grandma her coffee now. I'll come back in a while, if ever Bella comes back.' She took the cup of coffee to the lounge and gave it to her grandma. 'I'll go and get you some paper and things now while you drink that.'

'Thank you, dear. Very kind of you.'

Sophie ran up to her father's study and found the paper and pencils. She noticed the top drawer was slightly open and wondered why. She pulled it open some more and saw the cheque-books in there, not in their usual serried ranks but in something of a mess. She looked at the one on top and saw it was her grandma's. Surely Bella wouldn't have . . . no. Not even Bella was that unscrupulous, surely?

She pushed the drawer closed again and went downstairs, left the paper on the hall table, and went to look in the scullery for the board for Nellie to rest on. She wondered whether to tell her mother about her suspicions, but decided to keep them to herself. Paula had enough worries on her mind.

'There you are, Grandma. Paper and pencils and something to rest on.'

'Thank you, dear. I have to design some plates for Bella to sell to the company. I'm not sure how many she'll want. I didn't even know she worked for anyone in the industry, did you?'

'No. I'm not sure what she said to you.'

'She thought I could do some designs to sell to the company she works for.'

'Perhaps she has some idea of where you can sell to. But she works for a company that designs clothes. We both do, actually.'

'Oh, does that mean you can make me a new dress for the party?'

'I'm not really sure about that.'

'If she can sell my designs, it will help pay for some of the things the family needs. There isn't much money left, you know.'

'I know. But it's nothing you have to be concerned about. Now, shall I rest the board on the arms of your chair?'

Soon Nellie was happily drawing, and Sophie left her. She took the cup back to the kitchen and sat on one of the stools to chat to her mum.

'How's she getting on?' Paula asked.

'No idea. Bella's told her some tale about selling her drawings to some company or other. She thinks she's about to save the family fortune. If it keeps her happy for a while, it doesn't matter, does it?'

'Not at all. Perhaps we may have to buy more paper, but that's nothing. I'd love it if she was capable of drawing something halfway decent. When I think of the designs she used to do . . . '

'She was amazing, wasn't she?' Paula nodded. 'Can I do anything to help? You've been stuck in here all morning.'

'I've made some more cake for tea. As long as I can keep Bella away from it till then, we'll be fine. I've actually quite enjoyed myself. Not having to keep going to look after Nellie is quite a rest for me. You go back to her now, dear. Oh, you could lay the table for me if you wouldn't mind.'

'Of course. I'll do it next and then go back to the lounge to see how Grandma's doing.'

The dining room was elegant, with a table large enough to seat a number of people. Sophie set it for five and put out mats in the centre. She assumed they'd be using vegetable dishes and her father would carve. She thought about the people who'd sat round this table in the past and the stories they could tell. Nellie's mother had been among them at one time, and she knew Nellie's brothers and sister had also been here. Paula was planning a tea party for them, too, so they'd all be there again. Sophie was keen to be part of that occasion. Perhaps she could take the Monday off work and come to help with the clearing up. She smiled and went back to the lounge.

'How are you getting on, Grandma?' she asked.

'Not very well. Wretched pencils keep breaking. Can you sharpen them for me?'

Sophie saw that most of the pencils were lying on the floor; several of them were snapped in two pieces and the rest had broken points.

'Oh dear, you've had a time. Perhaps you're pressing too hard.'

'You can't get the quality anymore. They never used to break like this.' Nellie broke the final one on her paper and threw it down. 'I'm sick of this. I need some stronger ones. Take it away.'

Sophie looked at the paper on the board. There were a series of deep holes and a few scribbles, but nothing more. She felt suddenly moved to tears as she collected the board from her grandma. She picked up the pencils and swept away the broken points from the old woman's lap. It was all so sad. However much she wanted to draw, they had to find some other way of making it possible.

'Don't worry about it, Grandma. I don't think Bella will mind at all.'

'But I've let her down. I hope she won't be cross with me.'

'Of course she won't. Now, why don't you try to have a little snooze? Then you'll be ready to enjoy your lunch. I think Mum's made an apple pie for pudding.'

'Oh how lovely. We don't very often have proper puddings these days.'

'I'm sure you do.'

'Not apple pie though.'

'Possibly not.'

'When's Bella coming to see me? She said she'd be able to come more often.'

'When she gets back from her walk. She shouldn't be long. Close your eyes now and try to snooze.' Obediently, Nellie closed her eyes and looked as if she were going to sleep. Sophie sighed and took the drawing things away with her into the kitchen.

'That was a total waste of time,' she

said to Paula. 'She kept breaking the pencils. Shall I throw these away?'

'I suppose so. The others will sharpen again, won't they?'

'I'm sure they will. I'll take them back to Daddy's study. If I leave them on top of his desk, do you think he'll see them?'

'Of course. I'll tell him what happened.'

'Mum . . . I . . . Oh, it's nothing. Never mind.' She had been about to mention Grandma's chequebook and Bella's possible meddling, but decided not to. 'I'll take them up. The table's laid ready.'

'Thank you, dear. I'll put the vegetables on when your father gets back. What time do you need to leave this evening?'

'I think there's a train at five-thirty. In fact, I know there's a train then. I don't know if Bella will want to wait till then, though.'

'She certainly can. One trip to the station is enough for us on a Sunday.'

'Now if Bella had a car . . . ' She giggled.

'Now then, that's enough of that,' laughed Paula. 'Oh, it is good to have you here. You make such a difference to the place.'

'I'm glad. It's lovely to feel welcome.' She gave her mother a hug and went upstairs to her father's study.

Bella came back from her walk and went into the kitchen. 'I'm gasping for a drink. Have we got any wine open?'

'I believe William has a bottle ready for lunch,' Paula said.

'Oh goody. I'll help myself to a glass now.' She went into the dining room and saw the bottle of burgundy on the sideboard, poured a large glass, and topped it up again once she had taken a good swig. Then she went into the lounge and saw her mother was asleep.

'Oh, you're back,' said Sophie, coming into the room. 'What have you got there?'

'Only some wine. It's on the sideboard if you want some. Bring the bottle in here and we can share it.'

'I think that's for lunch, actually.'

'Well, it won't matter if we have some before lunch, will it?'

'I don't suppose there'll be any left at the rate you're going.'

'Oh don't be such a goody-goody.'

'Bella, how lovely you've come to see me,' Nellie said as she stretched and sat up.

'Of course I have, Mum. Just to see you.'

'I tried to draw something but the pencils kept breaking. Poor quality. Must get William to look into it.' Bella looked at Sophie questioningly.

'I found some, and paper for her to have a go, but she wasn't able to do it.'

'I'm sorry, dear, but I haven't done the designs you wanted. I will do some soon, though. I don't like to let anyone down.'

'You haven't, Grandma. Really you haven't,' Sophie was saying.

'But I have. Bella needed to take them into the factory tomorrow. She was going to sell them. Help out with the family's

114

money problems.'

'Mother, stop worrying about money,' Bella said. 'There's plenty of money in the bank. Now, I'm going to get myself a wee drop more wine.'

She left the room and Sophie gave a long sigh. Unfortunately for her, Bella was a problem that she was going to have to take back to the flat with her.

7

They all enjoyed their lunch. William was rather upset when he discovered his precious bottle of wine had been half-drunk before they'd even sat down. 'I won't offer you any, Bella, as you've drunk half a bottle of it already,' he snapped. She scowled at him but said nothing.

They all moved into the lounge and Sophie went to make coffee, insisting on Paula having a sit-down. 'Bella and I will clear up. Come on, Bella, take the dirty dishes out into the kitchen.'

Bella scowled again but did carry some of the plates out. 'I'm leaving soon. You'll have to do it yourself. I'll call for a taxi to take me to the station. But I'll have to get some money from my brother before I do. Unless you can lend me some?'

'No. Any money I have will have to

116

feed us for the week. I doubt you'll contribute anyway. You still owe me for last week's shopping.'

'Oh, well I'm a bit short this week. I'll pay you when we get paid.'

'That's two weeks away. I'm not sure what you intend to do till then.'

'I'll be fine, don't worry. I'll go and ask William to sub me now and then I'll be off.'

'What about the dishes?'

'I'll give you the pleasure of doing them, my dear. I'll be out this evening, so don't wait up.'

'Do you want coffee?'

'Yes, please. It'll take me a while to get William on board. Bring mine in with the rest.' She swung out of the room and left Sophie to do it all, as usual. She shook her head. It was definitely time to look for somewhere else to live. She felt she'd suffered enough. And if Bella thought she was going to provide food for her for yet another week, she could think again.

Sophie took the coffee into the lounge

and smiled sweetly at the assembled company. 'Here we are. Bella's leaving after this, but I expect she's told you. Are you going to pay for her, Dad?'

'I'm not sure what you mean.'

'Hasn't she asked you yet? She wants you to pay for her taxi to the station and for her ticket back.'

'Really? I don't have much cash in the house at present. I paid for the taxi yesterday and that used it up.'

'I'm sure you'd all like to be rid of me,' Bella remarked.

'I'll take you both to the station and I'll pay for your ticket, but that's it,' William told her. 'You've freeloaded on us quite enough for one weekend.'

'I don't know what you mean,' Bella said innocently. 'How have I done that?'

'Never mind. Sophie, I think you wanted to catch the five-thirty, didn't you?'

'That's much too late for me,' Bella said. 'I'm supposed to be out this evening, and I wouldn't be back in time.'

'I suppose I could go a bit earlier,'

118

Sophie offered. 'But I'm not sure what the times are before five-thirty.'

'You've got my offer,' William said.

Bella really had perfected her scowl, Paula thought.

'And I don't see why Sophie should give up her afternoon to accommodate you,' William added.

Nellie was sitting quietly, listening to the exchange. She really didn't like the atmosphere that seemed to surround the two girls. She couldn't remember this sort of argument going on in the past; but perhaps now they'd grown up, they had grown apart. Bella was continuing to argue and Nellie could stand it no longer.

'Bella, you really are a naughty girl. Please be quiet and stop this constant arguing. If William says he hasn't got any money in house, he can't give it to you, now, can he?'

Everyone fell silent and looked at Nellie in surprise. It wasn't often she said anything like that and they all looked a bit sheepish.

'Sorry, Mum,' Bella said. 'I'm just a bit worried about not having any money.'

'Don't you get paid?'

'Of course, but not for a couple of weeks.'

'And what have you done with your last pay?'

'It's all gone.'

'Then you need to plan better. Can you give her a cheque for ten pounds, William? She can make that last till her next payday.' Nellie then sat back and closed her eyes.

Paula sat with her mouth slightly open. Her mother-in-law had sounded extremely reasonable; coherent and very clear in her words and, seemingly, in her thoughts. Perhaps she had been putting on an act. Or maybe it was a temporary situation and she didn't have a serious disability. Perhaps the antibiotics were working after all. She planned to speak to the doctor again the next day.

'Very well,' William agreed, 'I will

write a cheque for Bella. And I'll pay for the ticket on my credit card, and that is it. Understood?'

'I suppose so,' Bella said. 'Can you make it fifteen pounds? I owe Sophie something for food.'

'Ten pounds was mentioned. That's what you'll get.'

'Sorry, Sophie. You'll have to wait to get paid back. Blame your father's meanness.'

'How much does she owe you, Sophie?'

'I dread to think. She's always running out of cash and hasn't paid her share for food in ages.'

'And how often do I stay in to eat your wretched food?' Bella snapped at her. 'Not a lot.'

'I won't comment,' Sophie responded. 'You're always picking at food in the fridge. But let's not argue anymore. Your mother doesn't like it.'

'I'll give you five pounds then, Bella, and another five pounds to Sophie. That seems fair, doesn't it?' William said.

Paula could have sworn that Nellie

smiled to herself. William went up to his study and came back with two cheques and gave the two girls one each.

'Thank you, Dad,' Sophie said. 'Very kind of you.' She folded it and put into her bag.

Bella snatched at hers and looked at it. 'Thanks for nothing much. That'll pay my bus fare to work for a day. I'm going to my room to pack.'

'What on earth are you going to pack?' Sophie asked. 'You didn't bring anything.'

'There are a few things I'll take back with me. Is there a suitcase I can use? Oh, they'll be in the old trunk room. Don't bother, anyone. I can manage by myself, as usual.'

'She really is a case isn't she?' Paula remarked after Bella had gone upstairs.

'I'm sorry I didn't do a better job of bringing her up,' said Nellie.

'Well, she went away to school, didn't she? And she does have a degree of autism, don't forget. You seem a lot better this afternoon.'

'I do feel a bit clearer in my head. Not so muddled as I have been.'

'Perhaps we should call the doctor and let him see you like this.'

'If you want to, dear. I really don't mind. Perhaps it might be from seeing Bella again. You know, I'd forgotten what an unpleasant woman she can be.' Nellie lay back again and seemed to want to go to sleep.

'I'll go and get on with the washing-up,' Sophie said.

'I'll come and help you,' Paula offered. 'We can chat while we do it.'

'If you're sure. You were working all morning. I wanted you to have a rest.'

Mother and daughter went into the kitchen and began to tackle the dirty dishes.

'What do you think about Grandma?' Sophie asked.

'She seems more lucid than she has been for ages. Long may it last, I say. It would be wonderful if she really is better, but I can't see how or why, unless it's the tablets the doctor gave her. I'll speak to him tomorrow and see what he thinks.'

'Funny to think of you here and doing the same things each day. I'll be at work and doing all the stuff there, and you'll be here, cooking lunch and doing the housework.'

'It's my role in life. Though I have been thinking about going back to school to teach again. It would certainly help with the expenses. Your father isn't keen, though.'

'It would be good for you. Why not see if there are any vacancies around here?'

'I'm not sure I could do it after so long. Besides, there's always Grandma to be looked after. No, I feel it's all a bit of a pipe dream. There, that's it, all done; and thank you for your help.'

'Not at all. I must be like you; cooking and housework come naturally. And Mum, I've definitely decided to move out of the flat. I can't stand Bella always expecting me to do everything.

I'll look around, and if you can help me that would be wonderful.'

'I shall consider it an investment.'

'Thank you. Thank you very much. I won't tell my beloved aunt till I find somewhere.'

'Good thinking. I really want you to be happy, and if I can help, then it's all to the good. Now, I'd better get tea ready if you're to eat before you leave.'

'Heavens. It's all food, isn't it?'

'Oh, I'll just put out what's left of the cake and some scones. And tea, of course. No sandwiches or anything much.'

'Sounds lovely.' Sophie collected a tray and piled cups and saucers and side plates on it.

'Do you want to give Bella a call?' Paula suggested. 'She'll only complain if she misses tea.'

Sophie went to the bottom of the stairs and called out. Bella came thudding down, clutching a large suitcase that was obviously heavy.

'Goodness, what have you got in there?' Sophie asked her.

'Just a few oddments. Things I might be able to sell. Don't look like that. They're all mine. I haven't taken anything of yours or anyone else's.'

'Tea's ready, anyway. Mum thought you might be hungry again. There's even some of the cake left after your attack on it yesterday.'

'Oh good. It was nice.'

After they had all eaten and drunk, Sophie went to collect her own luggage, and it was time for them to leave. At the station, William went to the ticket office and bought Bella her ticket to Leicester. He gave her a little cash to pay for the bus back to their flat and said his goodbyes. Then he gave his daughter a big hug and whispered to her to keep in touch. It was the end of another weekend.

When they arrived back at the flat, Bella went straight to her room, hauling the suitcase behind her. Sophie went into the kitchen and saw Bella's dirty dishes from her meal on Friday. She decided to leave them for her aunt to sort out, and sat down in front of the television and put it on. She felt exhausted for some reason and soon fell asleep. Bella came in and used the phone to call a friend.

'Jeremy? Hi. It's Bella . . . How many Bellas do you know? Bella Cobridge . . . Yes, I know it's been ages . . . Look, I need to pick your brains . . . No, I can't talk now. Do you fancy a drink? I was thinking if you can pick me up, we'd have time for a couple before time's called . . . Yes, tonight of course . . . You can't? Oh well, another time perhaps. Bye.'

'Are you going out?' Sophie asked, waking from her snooze.

'Not sure. Depends on who's around. I'll try someone else.' She dialled again. 'David, how are you? Do you fancy a quick drink? I'm suffering from family overdose. Yes, I'm just back from a weekend with mother and the rest of the tribe . . . Yes, I know . . . So what do you think? No? Oh well. Another time. Bye.'

'It's almost ten, Bella. Much too late for most people. In fact, I think I might turn in. There's nothing worth watching.'

'A wonderful end to an astounding weekend. An early night.'

'You might try it yourself. Then you'll be up early for work tomorrow, for once. What a surprise for everyone. I'm out tomorrow night, by the way. You'll have to fend for yourself.'

'Really? And where are you going?'

'Nowhere that would interest you.' She was planning to go flat hunting and didn't want to say anything yet.

'Very mysterious. I might be out myself, so the poor flat will be left on its own.'

'Oh — there are still your dirty dishes in the sink. You could perhaps wash them up. Night, night.'

'Can't be bothered. They can stay there.'

'Forever if you don't do them. I'm not doing them.'

'So forever it is, then.'

Sophie went to her room, cursing her aunt. How could she be so damned annoying? She simply refused to wait on her anymore. She could look after herself or starve. Tomorrow she would go flat hunting and then treat herself to fish and chips somewhere. Also, she would go and phone the estate agent at some point, perhaps from work, and then arrange her visits. She felt excited at the prospect and stayed awake for a long time.

* * *

The next day Sophie was up early and made herself some toast and coffee. She wasn't sure how much time it would take to phone the estate agent. She wondered whether to ask Fred to go with her but decided against it. He was a good friend, but he might find it a bit strange accompanying her to look for a flat. All the same, she decided she'd tell him about her plans. She heard Bella rising and staggering into the kitchen.

'Oh good, you've made some toast and coffee,' her aunt said. 'Very civilised.'

'Sorry, that's mine. There is some bread left, though not much. Excuse me,' Sophie said, reaching for her mug and plate of toast. She sat down and began to eat.

'I'll get something at work,' Bella decided. 'I'm going to the bank at lunchtime.' Sophie said nothing. 'Do you want me to pay your cheque in too?'

'Thank you, but no. I'll pay it in later in the week.'

'Suit yourself.' Bella drifted out again, and Sophie finished her toast and got ready to leave. She called out her goodbye and walked down the road. It was a lovely morning, so she decided to walk to the next bus stop. She had plenty of time and felt like making the most of the day.

A car stopped beside her. It was Fred. 'Have you missed your bus?' he asked.

'No. It was such a nice day, I thought I'd walk a bit.'

'Do you want a lift?'

'Thanks, I'd love to ride with you. What are you doing in this part of town? I thought you lived near Wigston.'

'I've recently moved. Got my own flat now.'

'How lovely. Where's that?'

'In the new block not far from you. They're really nice. All bright and shiny.'

'Are they all taken? Only, I'm thinking of buying somewhere to live on my own too.'

'There are still one or two left, but they're getting snapped up very quickly.'

'I can phone for an appointment today. How exciting.'

'Look, why not come and look at my place? It'll give you an idea of what they're like. If you're interested, you can go to the agent and see what's left.'

'That would be wonderful. Thank you.'

'We could go round at lunchtime if

you like. Depends how quickly you want to move. But hang on, I thought you had a place already?'

'Bella lives there with me. That's just too much for anyone to bear. Are the flats very expensive?'

'Well, I suppose they are.' He told her the cost. She wasn't sure if it would be too much for her mother to spend. But this seemed like such a good deal.

'I'll phone home and see what my mother says. I'm afraid it may be too much for her.'

'You could always take out a mortgage to top it up.'

'I'm not sure. I doubt the family would be willing to allow me to do that.'

'Really? My family seemed quite relieved to be rid of me. Well, not really. But my parents were delighted with the place. Let's see what you think of it. I'll pick you up at lunchtime. I'll even make you a sandwich at my place.' He parked the car near the exit so they could make a swift getaway later.

'Thank you, Fred. And thanks for the lift.'

'It could become the normal thing if you move into my block of flats. I could bring you to work every day. Ah well, back to the grindstone. Have a good morning.'

'Thanks. And you.'

Sophie went into her work area and saw she was the first to arrive. She rushed to the phone and dialled her parents' number. 'Mum? I've got to be quick. I'm phoning from work. Look, there's a chance of me getting a brand-new flat, but it's expensive. I just wanted to check with you before I looked at it.' She told her the price.

'If it's really everything you want, I'll go to that amount,' Paula said. 'But please, make sure it's perfect for you. When are you going to look?'

'Fred's just moved in, and he's taking me there at lunchtime. Have to go now. Million thanks, and for the weekend as well. Love you. Bye.' She put the phone down as Mr Hill came in.

'Who was that?' he asked.

'Wrong number. Someone wanting the swimming pool,' she lied.

'How's the evening dress coming along?'

'Nearly finished, I think. I'll go and check.' Her day had begun properly. She had done several different jobs by the time Bella arrived.

'Can you check on the progress of the evening dress?' Bella asked her.

'Done that. It'll be finished by the end of the morning.'

'Oh, right. How's it looking?'

'Gorgeous. I think you'll love it. Mr Hill's impressed, anyway.'

'Really? Does he know you designed it?'

'No, you're still safe.'

'Okay, I'll start on the next project then. Make me a coffee, will you? And get one of those bun things I like.'

'Money?'

'I'll pay you back when I've been to the bank.'

'Typical.' Sophie went off to buy the

bun and then made coffee. No 'please' and never a 'thank you' from Bella. She sighed. If she did move out, she'd still have to wait on her hand and foot in the works. Still, it would be better. Anything would be better.

When lunchtime came round, Fred came to collect Sophie. She didn't say anything to anyone and Bella asked where she was going. Sophie pretended not to hear, and the pair ran down to his car. Ten minutes later, he parked in the generous car park area and they went into the building. His flat was on the first floor, so they walked up the stairs. She felt ridiculously excited. This was the first stage of her new independence.

'Come on in,' Fred said. 'This is rather a small hallway, but turn right and that's the lounge,' he said.

It was a reasonably sized room, rather sparsely furnished but with a nice carpet and a largish sofa. Sophie went over to the window and looked out at a garden. 'Whose is the garden?'

'It's communal. We have to pay

charges, and someone keeps the lawns mowed and the corridors cleaned each week.'

'And is this the kitchen?' she asked, pushing the door open.

'Yes, but you'll have to excuse the mess. I haven't tidied up. I didn't know I'd be bringing you here.'

'It's lovely. I like the bench along the side. I suppose you can sit there to eat?'

'I usually eat in front of the television, I have to admit. But yes, one could eat there. As long as you don't invite too many people at once.' They both laughed.

'I like it a lot. Is there just one bedroom?'

'Er, yes. I haven't actually made the bed. But well, have a look if you want to.'

Sophie smiled and pushed open the door. It was a bright, airy room, again sparsely furnished, but very nice.

'And a bathroom? That must be opposite the entrance. May I take a peek?'

The poor man looked rather embarrassed but nodded his agreement. It was a nice enough room, and Sophie thought the whole place would really suit her. 'Thank you very much for showing me round,' she said to him.

'I'm sorry it's a mess. I would have tidied up if I'd known you were coming round.'

'Don't worry. You said there are several more places for sale — how do I get to see them?'

'I'll find the number for you to call. Perhaps you can arrange it for this evening. What do you think?'

'Sounds like a plan.'

'I can always give you a lift, and you can come and wait here. If you want to, of course.'

'You really are very kind. Thank you. I haven't even eaten my sandwiches yet.'

'Nor me. Let's eat them now.'

When they had finished, Sophie said, 'I suppose we should get back to the fun factory now.'

'Okay, and perhaps I can stop some-where for you to phone.' He looked in a drawer and found the number of the estate agent. 'Afraid I don't have a phone yet.'

'Don't worry, I can always call from work. Mr Hill won't mind if it's just a local call. How exciting. My own flat.'

8

Bella had gone out to the bank. Her precious cheque was burning a hole in her pocket; she wanted to pay it in, and then she could go and look at cars. She also had William's paltry cheque to pay in. Inside the bank, she filled in the form and handed it to the counter clerk.

'I'd like to draw something out. Twenty pounds should do it.'

'I'm sorry, madam, but you don't have twenty pounds in your account. In fact, you're somewhat overdrawn.'

'But I'm paying over five thousand in. Surely I can draw something on that.'

'The cheque has to clear first, I'm afraid.'

'Oh for heaven's sake. How can you be so pedantic?'

'I'm sorry, madam. It's the rules.'

'Rules, rules, rules. Let me see the manager.'

'I would, but I'm afraid he's at lunch. You can make an appointment for later this afternoon if you like. I'm afraid he'll only tell you the same thing. The cheque has to clear before you can draw out any money against it. It should clear by Friday.'

'And what am I supposed to do till then?'

'I'm sorry, madam. I can't help you.'

'Temporary overdraft perhaps?'

'You're overdrawn at present. I can arrange for you to see the manager if you like.'

'I need to get back to work now. But yes, please.'

The clerk looked in a diary to one side. 'You can see him on Wednesday at three-thirty.'

'Oh forget it. I'll come in on Friday.' She turned and left the bank, cursing broadly about desk clerks with no initiative. She hurried back to work and slumped down at her desk. How she hated being without enough money. Perhaps Sophie would lend her some.

She didn't like to ask her flatmate, but she was family after all, and Bella really couldn't go on like this. Still, by Friday she'd have plenty of money, and looked forward to selecting her new car.

Where was her niece, anyway? She wanted more coffee, or perhaps a cup of tea. She went and looked in the sewing room, but there was no sign of her. It never occurred to her to make her own tea, and she sat waiting for Sophie's return.

'Where have you been?' she demanded when Sophie walked in.

'Out. Why? Did you want something?'

'I'm gasping for some tea.'

'Why didn't you make it yourself?' Bella simply stared at her. 'Okay, I'll make it. But it's quite a simple operation, you know. I'll teach you sometime.'

'No need to be rude. It's part of your job to look after my needs, and that includes making tea. Now go along and do it.'

'A 'please' wouldn't go amiss. It's all

right, I'm going.'

Cursing her, Sophie went to make the tea. While she waited for the kettle to boil, she imagined what it would be like to live in one of the flats. She would need to get some furniture, but she could at least take her own bed and bedroom stuff. She wasn't sure how much money her mother was thinking about. Still, even if it meant she used camping chairs, she'd be very happy to move out from Bella's clutches.

She made the tea and poured a cup. She then decided she'd have a cup as well, and poured that too. No doubt she'd be in trouble with her aunt, but what the heck — she'd be moving out soon; and though she'd have to see her at work every day, at least she'd get her own life at home.

'Here you are,' Sophie said, plonking Bella's cup down on her desk.

'You're having one too? Hope you've put your money into the fund.'

'Nope. I thought I'd rely on you having paid.'

142

'You need to put some money in the pot. I'm a bit short this week, so it's down to you.'

'Sorry, I don't have any spare cash,' Sophie lied. 'And don't forget I'll be out tonight. You'll need to sort your own meal.'

Bella glared at her. 'Where are you going?'

'I told you. Out. You never tell me where you're going, so why should I tell you?'

'Sophie, what's come over you? Why are you being so . . . so belligerent? It's not like you.'

'There's only so far you can push a person, you know. I think you must realise you've reached your limit.'

'But why? What have I done? I've been perfectly normal with you, haven't I?'

'That's the problem. Your 'normal' consists of bullying me, or trying to. You take me totally for granted. You expect me to get your meals ready, and if you don't like what I've provided, you turn your nose up and decide to go out. And your behaviour this weekend . . . well, that just about took the biscuit.'

'I don't know what you're talking about. I did what you told me and went to see the family. I might not have been exactly welcome, but I hope I've sown a few seeds. They need more help. Mother is in a bad state and Paula can barely cope. They also need a full-time cook. I've told my brother to sort it.'

'I don't think it's that simple. Money's a bit short.' Sophie felt guilty at this point, knowing her mother was about to give her some money to buy a flat. Paula could have used money to make her own life easier.

'Nonsense. They've got all the money from selling the factory. And their house must be worth a small fortune. I really don't buy into their poverty. Now, go and see how they're getting on in the sewing room. That evening dress should be finished by now. I want to see if I can approve it before the boss comes along to inspect it.'

Sophie escaped and went to the sewing room. Her own design was almost finished and was looking lovely. 'That's gorgeous, Mary,' Sophie enthused when she saw it. 'You've done such a good job on it.'

'Thanks, Sophie. I love the design. Much less fussy than her usual stuff. You should try it on. Show her how good it looks.'

'Oh, I couldn't.'

'Course you could. Go and try it now. I'll come and fasten it along the back.'

'I don't have shoes or anything.'

'Go on.'

'Yes, go on Sophie,' chimed in one of the other ladies. 'We'd all like to see it.'

'Well, okay then. I'll go behind the curtain and you can see what it looks like.' She went there with the dress, slipped off her skirt and jumper, and put the blue creation over her head. It hung down and settled perfectly over her body. 'Come and fasten me up then, Mary,' she called.

'It looks wonderful!' Mary gushed. 'Turn round.'

Sophie was soon fastened in. She looked in the mirror. 'It does look good,' she admitted.

'Come and show the others,' Mary encouraged her.

Shyly, Sophie stepped out from behind the curtains to calls of 'Lovely,' 'Perfect,' and 'You should wear it.'

'You should go and show Bella,' Mary said.

'Oh no, she'd probably tell me off for trying it on.'

'I'll go and fetch her in here.'

'Go on, then. If she sees it in here, she won't say too much.'

A few moments later, Bella came in looking grumpy. 'What's the problem?'

'No problem,' Mary said. 'We thought you'd like to see the dress.'

Bella looked at Sophie and drew in her breath. It did look stunning. Not at all Sophie's usual style, but she had to admit, it really worked well.

'Turn round so I can see the back,'

Bella said. Sophie did. 'Not bad. Okay, you can take it off now.'

'Congratulations, Bella,' Mary said. 'It's different from your usual stuff, but we all love it.'

'I'm glad,' Bella replied. Sophie stared at her, but Bella said nothing more. She went back into her office and Sophie went to change. At this point, Mr Hill came in.

'How's the dress getting on?' he asked.

'Sophie, come out and show him,' Mary called. 'She was modelling it for us to see.'

Sophie came back out and Mr Hill looked at the dress, turning her round to view the back. 'That is lovely,' he commented. 'Very different, and I think it looks perfect. It fits you very well too, Sophie. I think you should join the modelling team, actually. Be quite handy having you here.'

'Thank you,' Sophie replied. 'But I don't think I could join your team. I haven't got enough time for all the make-up and other stuff.'

'I like your simple look. I think you could do very well. Next time we have the need to demonstrate our lines, I shall call on you.'

'If I'm not making tea or something,' she muttered.

'What on earth are you talking about?' Mr Hill demanded.

'Nothing. I'm sorry, I shouldn't have said that.'

'Who do you make tea for?'

'Bella, mostly. But forget it, please.'

'You mean to say she gets you to make her tea?'

'Only sometimes.'

'You admit it, love — she's got you on the hop all the time,' said Mary. 'Always got you running round after buns or something.'

'I shall have a word with her,' Mr Hill said. 'I don't want you acting as some sort of slave to her. I know she's a talented designer, but that's about it. She's not the hardest worker.' The last comments were made to Sophie alone, for which she was grateful. If Bella found out Sophie had said anything, she'd be furious.

Sophie went to change back into her work clothes and hung the lovely dress on a hanger. When she went back into the office she shared with her aunt, she walked into one heck of a row. Bella was arguing madly with Mr Hill, and he was equally adamant that she was abusing her workmate.

'What on earth has she said?' Bella demanded. 'Because I'd challenge that. I don't treat her as some sort of slave. I'm always perfectly normal with her and give her a lot of responsibility.'

'How often does she make your tea?'

'Oh I don't know. Sometimes, perhaps.'

'And fetch you buns?'

'Hardly ever.'

Sophie went to her desk and said nothing. She took out some of Bella's designs and started to work on them.

Mr Hill ceased his ranting and shook his head. 'I don't know. Just watch yourself, Bella. You're not indispensable, you know. I think with a bit of training, young Sophie here might well be capable of doing her own designs.'

'Really, Mr Hill, I don't think so,' Bella retorted. 'She has some talent, but not for actual design.' She glanced across at Sophie, as if challenging her not to say a word. She didn't, and Bella nodded. 'Is there anything else?' she asked, smiling sweetly.

'I don't think so,' Mr Hill said. 'Remember what I said about modelling, Sophie. I shall call on you at the appropriate time.'

'Thank you, Mr Hill. I think I'd probably like that.' He smiled at her as he went back to collect the evening dress.

'What's this about modelling?' Bella asked.

'He wanted me to model the dress sometimes. I doubt he'll remember, anyway.'

'And is that where he got the idea I use you as a slave?'

'I really don't know. Now, if you'll excuse me, I need to work on the pattern for your latest collection.' She thought about the phone call she'd made on her way back. She had arranged for the agent to meet her at six o'clock and could hardly wait. She usually finished work at five-thirty, and that would allow her plenty of time. Fred had offered to drive her back, and she could wait in his flat. At almost five-thirty, she started to pack up her things.

'Where are you going?' asked Bella.

'Out.'

'Not yet you're not. Have you finished the work you were doing?'

'Nearly. I'll finish it in the morning.'

'I want it done now.'

'I'm sorry, but I'm going to leave on time. I'm getting a lift and he'll be waiting.'

'He? Who are you going out with?'

'It's no business of yours,' Sophie told her.

'But you're leaving before you've

finished your tasks. Hardly going to impress your new friend Mr Hill, is it?'

'Don't be so difficult, Bella. You're cross because I happen to be going somewhere without you. Now if you'll excuse me, I shall be late.'

'You can't go. I won't let you.' Bella stamped her foot angrily but Sophie wasn't listening. She put on her coat and left the office.

Down in the car park, Fred was waiting impatiently. Sophie apologised and got into the car. 'Sorry. Bella was throwing a hissy fit. We shall be in time, won't we?'

'Course we will, love. It's only a short drive. I can't wait for you to move in. It'll be terrific to have you near to me. Sorry, I'm being presumptuous.'

'Not at all. I'm glad you'll like having me near, if I'm honest. It'll make a change from Bella ranting on all the time.'

'I can't think why you live together, actually.'

'Largely because my dad bought us

the flat. I don't think he realised what she'd be like.'

'Isn't she your aunt or something?'

'Yes, she's my dad's sister. Loads younger than him, of course. She's always been difficult, but never as bad as she is now.'

'Well, here we are. And if I'm not mistaken, that's the agent sitting in his car.'

'Oh dear. I must be late.'

'Not at all. He's early. Best of luck.'

'Thanks. And thanks for the lift.'

'Come and tell me how you got on, won't you?'

'Well, yes, okay. If you really want me to.'

'Course I do.'

Sophie got out and crossed to the agent's car. He got out as she approached and held out a hand. 'I'm Michael from Star Properties. Pleased to meet you, Miss Cobridge.'

'Pleased to meet you too, Mr . . . er, Michael.'

'We have four flats in the block

currently for sale. I'm sure one of them will be exactly what you're looking for.' He led the way in through the same door Fred had used. 'The first one is on the ground floor. Are you happy with that?'

'I don't see why not.'

'It's just that some women don't like being on the ground floor. Security, you understand.'

'Oh, I see. Let's look at it anyway.'

It all smelt so new, Sophie thought. It was identical to Fred's place, with a different coloured carpet. The kitchen and lounge room were just the same, and the bedroom and bathroom looked over the garden. It really was very nice, and Sophie loved it. But there were more flats to see, so she asked Michael if they could move on.

'Certainly,' he said. 'The next one is up a floor.'

They walked up the same stairs she'd walked up earlier that day, and at the top they turned and walked across the landing. Michael opened the door and they went inside. Sophie went to look out of the window and could see the garden.

'I think I prefer this one. The garden view is better from the lounge than the bedroom.'

'I agree. The other two flats are near the other staircase. They're all alike, except one of them has two bedrooms. More expensive, of course.'

'I don't really need two bedrooms, but I'll take a look anyway.'

'Very well. Do you want to see the bedroom?'

'I'll have a glance.'

She poked her nose round the door, and also into the bathroom. Then they went down the stairs again and round to the other side of the building. Michael led the way in through the other door.

'Again, it's one downstairs and one upstairs.'

Thinking about it, Sophie wondered if it might be too close to Fred if she lived next door to him. She really liked him, and felt he liked her, but if it didn't work out between them it could be difficult. On the other hand, she liked the next-door flat much better than either of the other two. She didn't feel her mother would want to pay the extra for two bedrooms, and otherwise it meant living on the ground floor.

'I need to discuss this with my mother before deciding,' she told Michael. 'But you can take it that I shall buy one of the flats.'

'That's fine. Only trouble is, I shall be bringing more clients round tomorrow, and they may choose the same flat that you like best.'

'I'll phone her tonight and call you tomorrow.'

'Splendid. Can I drop you anywhere?'

'No, thanks. I'm going to see a friend now. But thank you for your time.'

'My pleasure. You have my number, don't you? Oh, I should give you a brochure.' He opened his briefcase and handed her a glossy booklet.

'Thank you. I'll be in touch.'

He drove away as she watched, and then she went back to Fred's flat. She knocked on his door and he opened it almost before she had finished.

'Come on in,' he greeted her. 'What did you think?'

'I love them. I need to speak to my mum, though. I do actually like the one next door to you.'

'Terrific. That would be so good, having you right here.'

'I'm not sure if it *is* such a good idea, Fred. I mean, suppose we fell out. It could be awkward. Well, couldn't it?'

'Maybe. But why do you think we might fall out?'

Oh, I don't know. Just a thought.'

'Would you like to stay for some supper? I'm no great cook, but I can manage to heat up a pie and do some vegetables with it. What do you say?'

'Really? Well, thank you. I had planned to buy fish and chips on my way home. I told Bella I was going to be out for supper.'

'Unless you're desperate for fish and chips, why not stay here? I can run you home again afterwards.'

'Thank you very much. That would be lovely.'

'Sit down and I'll get you a drink. I've got some wine, but that's about all.'

'Thanks. That would be great.'

Fred went into the kitchen and Sophie heard the clattering of pans. Then she heard him open a bottle of wine and pour some into glasses. She felt slightly odd just sitting there and wanted to go and join him. Perhaps she could help prepare vegetables or something. She was about to get up when he came back with two glasses of wine.

'It's red. Hope that's okay?'

'Great, thank you. Can I help in the kitchen?'

'No, all under control. I sort of assumed you might stay, so I'd already put the pie in, and peeled potatoes. If you hadn't stayed, I'd have eaten the same meal again tomorrow.'

They shared a pleasant evening, and

it was almost nine-thirty before they realised it.

'I really need to go back,' Sophie said. 'I'm sorry; I don't know where the time went.'

'I'll get my keys and drive you,' offered Fred.

'I can easily walk,' she protested.

'Nonsense. I could let you walk back, but not at this time of night. Now, you'll have to tell me exactly where you live.'

She thanked him and told him her address. They reached the flat in minutes and she got out. 'Very kind of you. I've really enjoyed this evening.'

'The first of many more, I hope.'

Sophie grinned as she ran upstairs to her flat. It felt like the start of something special, and she hugged herself. She let herself in, expecting Bella to be out somewhere.

'Whatever time do you call this?' her aunt immediately challenged.

'Er, quarter to ten. Your watch stopped?'

'Where on earth have you been till now?'

'Out with a friend. Had a lovely evening.'

'Lucky you. I haven't even had a thing to eat. The cupboards are bare.'

'Oh dear. You didn't stop on your way home to get anything?'

'I don't actually have any cash. The bank wouldn't let me have anything despite the cheques I paid in.'

'I'm sorry to hear that.'

'I don't suppose you could lend me some for a few days?'

'Sorry. I've only got enough to last me to the end of the week.'

'What am I supposed to do? I need some money. Please, Sophie. Just a few quid. I can pay you back on Friday.'

She felt sorry for her aunt and looked in her purse. 'I can let you have two pounds, but that's all.'

'It'll have to do. Thanks. Are you out tomorrow, or will you be here to cook?'

'Not sure yet. I need to make a phone call. If you'll excuse me.'

'Who to?' Bella asked, but Sophie was already out in the hall by the phone. Then she hauled it into her room and shut the door. She certainly didn't want Bella to hear her conversation with her mother. She dialled the number and Paula answered.

'I've seen the flat, Mum. It's gorgeous. I have to call back tomorrow if I'm going to buy it.'

'Are you sure it's what you want? I mean, it's the only one you've seen.'

'I did see four. They were all the same except one which has two bedrooms. But that one is more expensive. Oh Mum, it's just what I want. All new and clean. I shall be one of the first people living there.'

'I think your father and I would like to see it first. Before I send you the money, I mean.'

They talked for a while about the logistics of them making the trip and finally agreed. They would arrange for someone to look after Nellie and would come to Leicester on Thursday. Sophie would take the day off work, assuming her boss would agree, and they could all go round to look at the flat. Sophie put the phone down and sat smiling to herself.

9

The improvement in Nellie's health seemed to continue during the week. Paula could hardly believe it when she could have relatively normal conversations with her and she wanted to join in with ordinary activities.

'She really does seem back to her old self,' Paula said to William one evening. 'I don't know why or how, but I think she might cope with a discussion about moving.'

'We could give it a try. If she's able to talk sensibly, perhaps we can start looking for places. I wonder why she seemed in such a bad way before.'

'I suspect Bella knocked it out of her. Or perhaps she really did have an infection of some sort. Anyway, she does seem much better, so I'm just going to enjoy that. And I've had a call from Sophie. I'd like to go and look at the new flat she wants. I said we'd go on Thursday. What do you think?'

'What, all the way to Leicester and back? I'm really not sure about that.'

'I feel it's essential if I'm going to buy the flat. It's not that I don't trust her, but I'd like to see where she's going to live. It's only about an hour and a half hours to drive there. I can go on my own if you don't want to go. You can stay and look after your mother.'

'You can't possibly drive all that way on your own. No, I'll come with you.'

'Jolly good. I'll get someone to come in and look after Nellie. It really would be too much for her to come with us.'

When Nellie heard of their plan to visit Leicester, she told them in no uncertain terms that she wanted to be included in the trip. 'I'd like to see where the girls live. I've never been, you know.'

'We're going to see a new flat that Sophie wants to buy,' Paula told her. 'It might be slightly difficult to go there without Bella knowing.'

'Why do you want it kept secret?'

'Well, Bella isn't the easiest person to live with. Sophie wants a place of her own.'

'Yes indeed, I can understand that. She does have something wrong with her, you know. I can't quite remember what it is, but I know it was always a problem at school.' She sat looking puzzled for a while until she forgot.

'It'll be a long drive for you, Mum,' William warned her. 'I'm not sure you could cope. I'm not sure *I* can cope, actually. But I can't let Paula go on her own.'

'I've only got to sit in the car, for goodness sake.' Nellie was getting more and more insistent.

'We'll think about it. And you think about it, too. You've got a couple of days before we shall be going.'

'I'm not going to change my mind. Now I'm going to have a rest. I'll leave you two to talk some more.' She rose from the breakfast table and went into the lounge.

'I'm going to the golf club,' William said almost inevitably. 'Back for lunch.'

Paula sat thinking about the trip to see her daughter. She felt quite excited at the prospect. It would be lovely to have a day out for once, with a visit to see Sophie at the end of it. She wondered what Bella's reaction would be. No doubt there would be fireworks when she found out she was being left on her own. She really would have to alter her way of life. Paula suspected that Bella spent all her money when she got it and had none left by the end of the month. Sophie, on the other hand, was sensible and spent her money frugally. Her own background had instilled that habit into her.

Paula decided not to tackle the thorny subject of moving house themselves, certainly not until after Thursday's outing. With a small sigh, she cleared the breakfast things away and washed up. The cleaning lady, Mrs Evans, had arrived, and Paula could hear the vacuum cleaner buzzing in the hall. She went through to tell her of the trip on Thursday.

'If my mother-in-law decides to stay at home, I wonder if you could stay with her?' Paula asked. 'She says she wants to come with us, but I think it may be too much for her.'

'How is she now?' asked Mrs Evans. 'Only, I doubt I could manage her if she's as bad as she was.'

'Touch wood, she really seems remarkably good at the moment. This is only a possibility, as I say. She wants to come with us.'

'Okay. I'll stay for the day.'

'I'll leave food for you both, and something for supper in case we're delayed. We should be back by the evening, of course, but one never knows about traffic and hold-ups.'

'Very well, Mrs Cobridge. You don't need to worry about her. I'll do the cleaning round as usual and look after her in between.'

'Thanks very much.'

* * *

The following day, things were thrown into confusion by a rather disturbing telephone call for William. He, Paula and Nellie were sitting in the lounge after lunch when the phone rang.

'Mr Cobridge?' said the voice at the other end. 'This is the manager at Lloyds Bank. You did actually terminate the account belonging to Mrs Nellie Cobridge?'

'Yes indeed. She was no longer able to cope with it and so we amalgamated her account with mine. Why do you ask?'

'We've had a request for payment of a cheque for five thousand pounds on her account.'

'What?' exclaimed William. 'Who's the cheque made out to?'

'A Miss Bella Cobridge. It's with her bank in Leicester.'

'Oh good heavens. Who's signed the cheque?'

'Mrs Cobridge. Though I must say, it's a bit difficult to read. It may possibly have been forged.'

'Oh no. My sister has a lot to answer for. She was pestering me for a cheque so she could buy a car. She must have taken matters into her own hands. I'm sorry you've been troubled.'

'Well I can't cash it, I'm afraid, sir. You don't have sufficient funds in your account. Unless you wish to transfer money from your savings account?'

'Certainly not. You must tell the Leicester branch to cancel the cheque. Or send it back, or whatever it is you have to do. Goodness me, that's terrible. I'll certainly speak to her. Thank you for drawing it to my attention.'

'Very well, sir. I'll tell Leicester it's been refused. Goodbye.'

William put the phone down and stormed into the lounge.

'Whatever's wrong?' asked Paula.

'Mother, did Bella get you to sign a cheque?'

'I can't remember. I think she may have done. Yes, she did ask me to sign something. I remember her telling me to sign several times.'

'And did you read what it was?'

'It was a blank something or other. I think she may have said she would put some other writing in later. Why? What have I done?'

'She's tried to pay in a cheque for five thousand pounds. We don't even have that sort of money in the account. The bank manager's just phoned, asking me what he should do. I've told him to cancel it. She's been on about getting a car.'

'I do remember that much. She said she'd come and see me much more often.'

'She really is the limit. It's a good job she was so greedy. If it had been for less money, it might just have gone through. Fortunately, the manager is on the ball and called me in time.'

'My goodness, what a dreadful mess,' Paula said. 'When did she do all this?'

'I don't know. Sunday probably, when you were cooking and I was at the golf club.'

Paula shrugged. 'I don't know what

to say. I find it hard to believe she would do something like that. It's really wicked of her. She's got a good job, as well. What are you going to do, William?'

'I might just leave it to the bank to tell her. It'll come as a shock, but it might teach her a lesson.'

'Perhaps. I just hope it doesn't rebound on us in some way. We need to decide about tomorrow. Do you really want to come with us, Nellie?'

'I think so. Yes, I'll say I do.'

'Very well,' Paula said. 'I'll tell Mrs Evans she won't be needed. I'll pop out and do that right away.'

She drove round to see the cleaning lady and told her not to come the next day. She then went to do some shopping and bought a couple of things to take with them for the girls. Somehow she felt sorry for Sophie living with her aunt, and knew that food would be the best thing she could take. They'd probably treat their daughter to lunch, as long as Bella was occupied at work.

The following morning, Paula was up early. She felt excited and couldn't sleep, so she decided to go down and make some tea. As she sat in the kitchen, she thought about the phone call the previous day. It had disturbed her deeply. Then she heard a noise and looked round. Nellie came into the room and sat with her.

'I often used to come down here early,' the older lady said, 'before the housekeeper or cook were up. It was so peaceful before a busy day started.'

'It must have been difficult for you. I don't think I'd have liked to have a large staff to control.'

'I remember being a servant here myself.'

Paula smiled. She'd heard the story several times before.

'It was hard work,' Nellie continued, 'and the housekeeper was very strict with us girls. It was James who rescued me and saw my talent. All a long time ago.'

'You did very well for yourself. Now, are you going to get dressed? I must, too. Put on something comfortable for the journey. It'll be a long day for you. Do you want me to help you?'

'Of course not, dear. I can manage to dress myself at least.'

'That's good. It doesn't seem so long ago we thought you'd gone quite potty.' She laughed as she said it and realised it may have been a tactless mistake.

'I thought so, too. But you know, dear, I think it was some sort of infection. I feel all right again now.'

'I'm very glad you do. It was a bad few weeks.'

The pair went upstairs and dressed. Paula woke William and told him to get up as they needed to get on their way.

Soon they set off in William's car and drove to Leicester. It was an uneventful journey and they arrived at the girls' flat by noon. Sophie had decided to take the whole day off, and despite Bella's protests had managed to stay at home. She had cleaned round everywhere and wondered whether she should have got something in for lunch.

'Mum, Dad, and Grandma too! That's a real surprise. Do you want to come in, or shall we go out and get some lunch?'

'I'd like to use your facilities,' said Nellie somewhat pedantically.

'Come on in then, all of you.'

'I've brought you something for supper and something for tomorrow too,' Paula said, hugging her daughter.

'Oh thank you, Mum. That's very kind of you.'

They all decided it would be a good idea to use the facilities, and when everyone was ready they drove out to a pub nearby.

'I just hope we don't bump into Bella there,' Sophie said in a worried voice during the journey. 'I haven't yet decided how I need to tackle her.' She turned to Nellie. 'So, Grandma, how are you?'

'You know, dear, I feel very much better. It seemed as if the mist cleared on Sunday afternoon. I must have had an infection.'

Sophie looked at her mother for confirmation, and Paula nodded. 'It does seem she's better now — aren't you, Mum?'

'Amazing. I'm so pleased. You can park here, William.'

They all trooped into the pub and had a light lunch. Sophie was anxious to show them the flat and kept looking at her watch. 'We really need to go soon. The agent will be there and wondering what's happened to me.'

'Okay, love,' William said. 'Is it far?'

'Not too far. I really hope you'll like it. I love it. It's all carpeted, and the kitchen is really nice.'

'I'll go and pay for lunch and we'll be off.' William went to the bar and the rest of the family went out to the car.

They stopped outside the block of flats and Sophie saw the agent, Michael, sitting in his car. Despite what he'd said about someone else looking, he showed them all four of the flats.

'I like the larger one upstairs,' said William.

'Yes, but it's more expensive,' Sophie told him. 'And I don't really need two bedrooms.'

'You could always use the second bedroom as a study or a dining room, couldn't you?' Paula suggested

'Well yes, but I don't like to take more money from you than necessary.'

'I think you should go for that one,' her mother said. 'And don't worry about the cost. It's all within budget.'

'Well thank you. I was going to ask for a loan to buy some furniture. Not a huge amount. I'll bring my bedroom stuff from our flat, but the lounge — well, I shall need a sofa at least.'

'Right, well if that's settled, we'll tell the agent to get moving,' William said. 'Hopefully you can move in quite soon. I assume you agree, dear?' he asked his wife.

'Yes, it's lovely. I hope you'll be very happy there.' She even wiped a small tear from the corner of her eye.

'Thank you so much,' Sophie said again. 'I can't tell you what this means to me. I can hardly believe it. Just think, I was only talking about it at the weekend, and here we all are, looking and deciding already.'

Michael was tactfully waiting outside and was delighted when they told him Sophie was ready to buy.

'I'll send a cheque when you need it,' Paula told her daughter. 'In fact, I'll send it when I get home again so there won't be any delays.'

'That's wonderful, Mum. Bella will be furious, but it's too bad. She'll have to get used to managing on her own.'

'I don't want to hurry you, dear, but we should get on our way again soon,' William said. 'We can drop you at your flat and then we must get moving.'

'I shall need to use the facilities again,' wailed Nellie.

'We all will, Nellie,' Paula said. 'Don't worry about it.'

Once Sophie had finally waved them off, she laughed to herself and danced round for several minutes, delighted at the prospect of moving into her very own flat. Somehow this place had never seemed entirely like home to her. Perhaps it was Bella's influence that made her feel that way.

She looked to see what her mother had brought for their tea and took out two lovely pork chops. That should please her ladyship, she thought as she prepared to cook them. Then she reminded herself to remain calm, as she didn't want to tell her aunt the news about the flat until much later.

★　★　★

Bella had plans of her own for the evening. Once she had finished at work, she went to a local garage to look at cars. Tomorrow, she thought, she would have access to five thousand pounds. She intended to buy a car for about three thousand and keep the rest for running costs and other expenses.

'I'd like to look at a car,' she said to the salesman. 'I'm prepared to spend what it takes, so I want to good one.'

'Certainly, madam. If you'd like to step over here, I can show you several. I'm assuming you're thinking of a second-hand one?'

'What have you got in new ones?' she asked.

'There are several smallish ones.' He showed her a couple and she turned her nose up at them. They were really very small. Hang it all, she might as well go for a better one. She increased her purchase price and eventually decided on a brand-new middle-sized car for two and a half thousand.

'If I give you a deposit today, you won't cash it in before tomorrow, will you?' she asked the salesman. 'It will clear after tomorrow, but I do want to make sure the car is mine. When can I take it away?'

'Early next week, perhaps, madam?'

'Oh, but I was hoping to have it for the weekend. Can't you organise that?'

'If you can organise the insurance, we can work on it for late tomorrow.'

'Wonderful. I'll see you tomorrow with

the balance and my insurance details.'

'Thank you, madam. A pleasure to do business with you.'

'Perhaps someone can give me a lift home now?'

'Er, I'm not sure. I won't be able to leave for at least another half hour. And I don't think there's anyone else available.'

'Oh well, never mind. I'll walk. It isn't too far.'

She left the garage and almost bounced along the road. This was the end of her walking anywhere. Tomorrow she'd be driving along in her own car. She laughed as she went, feeling on top of the world. She'd really put one over on William, and felt thrilled. She hadn't yet decided whether to tell Sophie or not. It would depend on how she felt and what sort of mood she was in. She wondered what her niece had been doing on her day off. No doubt she'd been out shopping for yet more fabric or something.

Bella reached the flat and ran upstairs. 'Hi, Sophie. I'm back.'

'Are you staying in this evening? For supper, I mean.'

'What have you got?'

'Pork chops.'

'Lovely. Yes, I'll stay in for them. What have you been up to today?'

'Oh, you know. This and that.' She could hardly suppress her grin and went into the kitchen to hide it.

'I'm going to change,' Bella announced. 'I'm exhausted. It's been one pig of a day.'

'Glad I missed it.'

'Mr Hill was in most of the time, messing around with my designs. By the time one of them was ready to make up, it looked nothing like what I'd put on the paper. But hey ho, I suppose it's par for the course really.'

'How long before you're ready to eat?'

'Not long. I'm starving, so I'll be quick.'

'Don't break your neck. It'll take a while to cook.'

When dinner was ready, the two of them sat at the kitchen table and ate their food.

'That was great,' Bella said. 'Why don't you buy something like that more often? I can't stand the mince you're always getting.'

'If you paid your share I'd buy stuff like that much more often.'

'I'll give you some cash tomorrow. I'll be quids in by then.'

'Really? We don't get paid for ages yet. Well, another week and a half at least.'

'Don't you worry. Leave it to Auntie Bella. I'll be able to give you a lift home from work after tomorrow, too.' Sophie looked at her in astonishment. 'What, you don't believe me? I've just bought myself a brand-new car. I'm collecting it after work tomorrow.'

'How? I mean, how can you afford it?'

'Ways and means, my girl. I shall go to the bank at lunchtime and draw out some cash, as well as a cheque to pay for the car.'

'Goodness. Well, best of luck with it. Now we'd better wash up. Do you want to wash or dry?'

'I'll leave it all to you. I'm going to watch television.'

'Typical.' But not for much longer, Sophie told herself with a big smile on her face, as she thought of her lovely new flat.

10

As they drove back to the Potteries, Paula commented on the flat they'd just seen. 'I thought it was lovely, didn't you both? I really think she'll be happy there.'

'I'm still not sure why she wants to leave the flat she has now,' Nellie said.

'I think it's because Bella doesn't do anything regarding the upkeep of the place and never cooks or anything. She's a real pain to share with.'

'I'm not really surprised. I'm sorry I didn't do a very good job with her upbringing,' Nellie moaned. 'She always was difficult.'

'You were busy,' William chipped in, 'running the factory and designing stuff.'

'Yes, I know, but *you* turned out all right.'

'Different circumstances. Dad was

alive most of my life. I did have my moments, though. I remember going to the States and learning my lesson, well and truly.'

'I never did hear what happened to you,' Nellie said.

'I lost all my money and my passport, and had to work my socks off to get home again. It was the making of me, actually. I came back ready to learn and start again.'

There was silence for a while, then suddenly William spoke again. 'We've been thinking of moving house, Mother. We've had a decent offer for Cobridge House, one that would enable us to buy a modern place and have some money left to live a decent life. What do you think?'

There was a silence from the back of the car. Paula turned to see if Nellie had fallen asleep, but she was obviously considering what her son had said. At last she spoke.

'I seem to remember you asking me this once before, somewhere in the fog of the past. Do you really want to say goodbye to everything we've known all our lives?'

'Well, yes,' he said. 'It's such a huge house. I don't really see how we can keep it going for much longer. Half of it is never used anymore.'

'Then I think we should start to look for somewhere else.'

Paula was amazed. 'Really? You'd actually agree to us finding a new place?'

'I don't see why not. I'd like it to be in the same area. A nice modern place would certainly have its advantages. Yes, let's start looking.'

'That's terrific,' William enthused. 'I'll phone the estate agent in the morning, see what he's got available, and we'll begin our search.'

'I think seeing the modern flat that Sophie wants to buy, well, that clinched it for me,' Paula said happily.

'Oh dear, you're not thinking of a flat, are you?' Nellie said with trepidation. 'I could never manage the stairs every day.'

'You manage the stairs at home,' Paula said.

'I think we should look for a bungalow. Save me all the hassle of going up and down all day. Do you know of any bungalows, dear?'

'Not at the moment,' laughed William. 'I'm sure we shall find something quite quickly. I'll also contact the company who made us an offer on the house; make sure they're still interested. I feel this is very much the start of a new beginning. Who knows, I might even find a new job.'

The rest of the journey passed quietly, all of them planning their new lives. Paula was thinking that she might even go back to teaching, and William was thinking of a new job. Nellie was thinking of the past and all the parties they had enjoyed in James's day. But that part of her life was now well and truly over. She needed to think of the future.

When they were nearly home, Paula suggested they stop and buy fish and chips for supper.

'Really?' William asked.

'Yes, really. We haven't had them for ages, and it will certainly save me cooking from scratch.'

'Well, if you're sure. Where should we go, then?'

'There's a place near home. Stop there, and I'll go and buy them.'

He pulled up outside the fish and chip shop and Paula went inside. She relished the wonderful smells and watched as the owner put battered fish into the hot fat. Her mouth was watering as she waited for her turn. The food was wrapped in newspaper and she carried it out to the car.

'I can't wait to get home,' she laughed. 'Best part of the day. Reminds me of when I was little and Mum used to buy this on a Friday night.'

'I can't remember the last time I had fish and chips,' Nellie said. 'I suppose it was many years ago. I hope you haven't bought me too much. I could never eat a whole portion.'

'Course not. Now you go inside, and I'll go and serve everything onto plates. I suppose you do want plates?' She'd have loved to eat hers from the paper.

'Of course we want plates. And knives and forks,' William replied stuffily.

'All right, I was joking. I won't use the vegetable dishes, however.'

William stared at her, wondering what she was talking about and missing her sarcasm completely.

★ ★ ★

In Leicester, Sophie and Bella were both up early. Much to Sophie's surprise, Bella was ready to go to work at the same time as she was.

'So what brought this on?' Sophie asked as they were waiting for the bus. 'I can't remember the last time we travelled to work together.'

'It's going to be a good day. I'm getting my car this afternoon.'

'I still don't know how you can afford it.'

'Don't worry about it. As I said, ways and means. We'll celebrate with a meal out this evening. Why don't you book somewhere special? My treat.'

'Let's wait and see. We can always book somewhere this evening. We're bound to find somewhere that'll take us.'

'As you like. Now, I need you to cover for me at lunchtime. I need to go to the bank and it may take me a while. Say I'm somewhere else in the factory if nosy old Hill comes looking for me.'

'We are entitled to our lunch break.'

'Yes, but as I say, I may take a while longer than usual.'

'All right then. I'm always covering for you anyway. Don't know what's so special about today.'

'Because it's my day for buying a brand-new chariot that will carry me anywhere I want to go.'

Paula glanced down the road. 'At last, here's the bus.'

'Pay for me, will you, love? I'll pay you back later today.'

Sophie gave a sigh and bought two tickets.

Mr Hill was waiting for them when they arrived. 'Good, you're both here,' he said. 'I want you to come down and model the evening dress this morning, Sophie.'

'Oh goodness, I haven't got shoes suitable for modelling,' she said in surprise.

'There are several pairs in the cupboard. I'm sure one of them will do.'

'How exciting,' she replied. 'When do you want me?'

'I'll call you in good time. I've got several buyers coming in today. I thought we'd put on a bit of a fashion show for them. And I'd like you to come down too, Bella. You can describe the design process to them. Talk a bit about where you got your inspiration.'

'OK, but it would be helpful to have an idea of what time you need us.'

'They're coming in at eleven, so perhaps if you come down then to get

191

ready. I'll talk to them first, of course — give them coffee and a spiel, and then we'll move into the area we use for our small demonstrations. You should be clear by twelve-thirty.'

'Oh, but . . . never mind.' Bella felt angry. She'd been planning to leave for the bank at twelve. At least Mr Hill wouldn't notice if she was late back, she consoled herself.

'Right, Sophie,' she said when Mr Hill had gone back to his office, 'where did you get the inspiration for the evening dress?'

'I don't know. I just drew it and it came out looking like that.'

'That'll never do for them. I'll have to make up something. Go and make me some coffee. I'll sit and think for a minute.'

'I will, but this is the last time I'm doing it. You make your own from now on.'

'Don't let this modelling go to your head for god's sake. It's only a tin-pot organisation, not a West End contract.'

'It's nothing to do with modelling. I'm sick of being bossed around by you. Sick of you taking the credit for my design.'

'Sophie, this isn't like you. Please don't go all prima donna on me.'

'I'm not. But from now on, you make your own coffee and buy your own buns.'

'I would, of course, but I haven't got any cash. Remember? You could go and buy us each a bun.'

'No thank you.' She swept out to make coffee for the woman she was growing to dislike immensely.

★　★　★

The fashion show was most successful in its way. Sophie was in and out of several dresses and Bella was commentating as she appeared. She hadn't realised she would be the only model and felt exhausted by the time she put on the evening dress. She walked through the curtains and was surprised at the gasp of appreciation and round of applause. Bella made few comments about it, saying it spoke for itself. Mr Hill was looking very proud of his wares and thanked the two women for their hard work. The buyers were almost queueing to make their purchases, many of them wanting to speak to the designer. Bella was hating every minute of being delayed and was almost bouncing on her heels to get away. At last she was released and shot out of the door as if being chased by wolves. Sophie hung up the various dresses and left the department.

Bella walked briskly along to the bank and asked to see the manager.

'Oh, *he* wanted to see *you*, madam,' said the desk clerk. 'Didn't you get his letter this morning?'

'Letter? What letter? No, I left home early today. The post hadn't arrived. Nothing wrong, I presume?'

'I'll tell the manager you're here. Please take a seat.'

She was shown into a small office at

one side of the counter, where the manager was waiting for her.

'Miss Cobridge. Please sit down.'

'What's going on? I've merely called for my money.'

'But it wasn't your money, was it, Miss Cobridge?'

'Not mine? Whatever are you talking about?'

'The cheque you paid in the other day. It turns out it was a forgery.'

'Don't be ridiculous.' The world started swimming around and she felt quite sick.

'It was written on an account that was closed some time ago. And the signature was very shaky. I suspect you got hold of an old chequebook and thought you'd forge a cheque made payable to yourself. I haven't yet called the police, but I shall do so before long.'

Bella went white. The police? He surely couldn't call the police! After all, she hadn't known the account was actually cancelled, had she?

'But my mother signed the cheque in good faith. She was quite happy for me to have the money. I've bought a new car. I'm supposed to collect it this afternoon. What am I going to say to the garage?'

'I'm sorry, madam, but there is no money for you to collect. You're overdrawn anyway. I understand you paid in a ten-pound cheque from your brother's account. That has gone some way to help with your deficit. When might we expect you to clear the overdraft?'

'How much is it?'

'Almost a hundred and fifty pounds. You don't have any arrangement with us, do you?'

'How on earth can it be that much? Are you sure?'

'Of course. Haven't you been receiving your statements?'

'I suppose so. But I never look at boring mail.'

'You would have also received several letters.'

'As I say, I don't look at things that bore me.'

'Well, I suggest you do in future.'

They discussed how she was going to clear her debts and she set up a facility for an overdraft. He'd also agreed not to call the police under the circumstances.

Feeling somewhat subdued, Bella went back to work. How on earth was she going to tell the garage about the car? And Sophie? The manager had allowed her a paltry five pounds, and she was supposed to make that last till next payday. Sophie would simply have to support her for the next week. She'd have to accept whatever her niece cooked and not complain. It was going to be a tough time ahead.

By the time Bella reached work, she realised she was very late. Oh well, she thought, Sophie would have covered for her. But Sophie was not in her office. Bella settled down to look at her drawings, but her mind was wallowing in her financial problems. Perhaps one of her men would help her out. Charlie, for instance. He was pretty well off. Perhaps he'd lend her enough money to buy a car.

By the time Sophie came back, Bella had cheered up considerably. 'Where have you been till now?' she asked.

'With Mr Hill. I'm sorry. He wanted you, but you weren't anywhere around. I went instead. He wanted information about manufacturing the dress. He's got several orders for it in different fabrics and colours. Naturally I was able to discuss it all with him. After all, I designed the thing in the first place, didn't I?'

'Did you tell him that?'

'No, but I think he may have guessed. I didn't say anything, though.'

'Well, thanks for that. Would you like some coffee? I've missed out on lunch, so I feel in need.'

Sophie was surprised. Obviously her speech that morning had borne fruit. 'Thanks. Yes, please.'

'How do you like it?'

'With milk. No sugar.' How had they been living together for so long and Bella was only just finding out how she liked her coffee? Her aunt came back with two cups. 'So, where do you want to go to eat tonight?' Sophie asked her.

'Er . . . I'm afraid there's been a change of plan. I won't be collecting my car after all.'

'Really? Why ever not?'

'Hold-up in finances.'

'Oh dear.' Sophie then remembered what her father had said yesterday, about something Bella had done that was so awful he didn't want to tell her. It was to do with money. Obviously, it was to do with money. 'You fiddled a cheque, didn't you? Was it one of Grandma's? Yes, I can see by your face. How could you? You really do take the biscuit. And Dad found out and stopped it. He said you'd done something so awful he wouldn't even tell me what it was.'

'Go on, rub it in. Anyway, when did he say it?'

'Well actually, they came over yester-day.'

'Nobody tells me anything. Why did they come?'

'To see me.'

'But you saw them at the weekend.'

Sophie looked away. She really didn't want to talk about her new flat, not when Bella was so upset about the car. 'Well, yes. They wanted a trip to Leicester. Leave it at that.' She escaped having to tell the truth by the timely arrival of Mr Hill.

'Bella, could you come to my office, please?'

'Certainly, Mr Hill. When do you want me to come?'

'Now, please.'

She rose and followed him.

'Sit down. I really don't think you're pulling your weight. Speaking to Sophie, I gather she does a lot for you. Includ-ing making coffee.'

'I've made her some today.'

'That's as may be. And the evening dress that is so successful — did you really design it?'

'Course I did.'

'I don't think you did, actually. I suspect that it was Sophie's work. It's quite different to your usual sort of thing.'

Bella looked at the floor, avoiding his gaze.

'Well?'

'All right, Sophie did do it. She did it when I was away one day. Satisfied?'

'Well thank you for that. I did tackle her about it, and she said it was your work. I'll have to have words with her for lying to me.'

'She probably did it for me. To save my skin.'

'Yes, I'm sure she did. And I'd like her to do some more designs. She's obviously got talent. Tell her I'll see her on Monday morning to discuss what's required.'

'What about me?'

'I'll have to think about it. Go on back now.'

Bella muttered under her breath as she went back to her office. How much longer would it be her office? she wondered. Today was proving to be the day from hell. She must go out this evening or she would go completely mad.

Back in the office she saw someone sitting on her desk, obviously talking to her niece. 'Can I help you?' she asked as she went in.

'Oh, no. I'm here to see Sophie.'

'Exactly who are you?'

'Fred's the name. I work in sales. Just popped by to see how things are with the lady.'

'I see. And how are things with the lady?'

'Fine, thanks,' Sophie answered. 'Fred's asked me out this evening. Hope you don't mind. We're going out to eat.'

'Lucky you.'

'What will you do, then, Bella?' Sophie asked.

'Haven't yet decided. I may go out. Depends on who's around. Now, are you going to do any more work today, or have you packed up?'

Fred raised his eyebrows and moved to the door. 'I'll call for you at seven,' he told Sophie with a grin.

'Okay, that's fine. Bye for now, Fred.' She returned his smile and then looked at Bella. 'How did it go with Mr Hill?'

'Nightmare time. He asked me outright if it was your design for the evening dress. Of course I said it was. No use pretending anymore.'

'Oh Bella, now he's going to know that I was lying to him.'

'He wants to see you Monday morning.'

'Oh lord, a whole weekend of worrying ahead. You should have said it was your design.'

'Just another event in my day from hell. I think I'm going to leave now. I can't do anything else today.'

'But there's another hour and a bit before it's time.'

'Today simply couldn't get any worse,' Bella insisted. 'I have to go to the garage and tell them I can't have my car. Or maybe I shouldn't go. What a decision.' She picked up her handbag and left the room. Sophie looked out of the window and saw her walking across the car park, looking somewhat defeated. She felt really sorry for her aunt and wondered if she was doing the right thing in leaving the flat. Maybe this was the lesson Bella needed to make her behave properly. Still, it was all her own fault. She had got herself into this hopeless situation, and no doubt she would be back to her own self before too long.

Sophie took out her work and continued until it really was time to leave. Monday was a while away, and she had this evening to look forward to.

★ ★ ★

Bella walked to the bus stop, all the time trying to make up her mind what to do about the garage. She decided she had better go, as they might try to cash her cheque. When she got to the garage, she noticed her beloved car sitting on the forecourt, then pushed the door open and went in.

'Ah, Miss Cobridge,' greeted the salesman she'd dealt with before. 'We've got it all ready for you.'

'I saw it. But I'm very sorry, my finances have failed to come through. I'm afraid I'm not going to be able to buy it after all. Well, not at the moment anyway.'

'I see. When do you think you will?'

'I simply don't know.'

'Do you want me to keep it for you? I mean to say, you did leave a deposit.'

'It's worthless. Tear it up. I'm sorry.' She turned away from him. She didn't want him to see her crying and walked out of the building. Somehow she didn't think Charlie would lend or give her that sort of cash. Miserably, she went back to the flat. It was too early to ring him yet to see if he'd take her out for the evening. She made a cup of tea and sat down to read the letter from the bank. It said pretty much what the manager had told her. She screwed it up and threw it into the bin in disgust. She was still sitting in the same position when Sophie arrived.

'You okay?' her niece asked.

'Not really. It seems the world is against me.'

'Oh dear, that sounds grim. I must go and change. Not sure what to wear actually. What do you think?'

'I really don't know. Or care, if it comes to that.'

'My goodness, you are in a state. What is it? The bank?'

'Mostly. I hate not having any money. Relying on the pittance I'm earning is really getting me down. And I have to pay off my overdraft. I don't suppose you — '

'No. I need every penny I'm earning.'

'Sorry, I shouldn't even ask. You've been so good to me, with all the cooking and cleaning and everything. I'm going to change. I promise you, I shall be the perfect flatmate from now on.' She reached over to Sophie and gave her a hug.

Sophie felt terrible. Disloyal, even. Perhaps she shouldn't move out after all, if her main reason for going was about to reform itself. Though it was probably a well-intentioned promise that could never be kept.

'I'd better get ready to go out now,' she managed to stammer.

'Hope you enjoy yourself. I may give someone a call later to see if they fancy an evening out.'

'Good. It might cheer you up a bit. You seem in need of it.' Sophie went into her bedroom and shut the door behind her.

Bella sat slumped in her chair for a while. She daren't even look in the fridge to see if there was anything she could eat. She would wait till Sophie had gone out, and look after that. She felt as low as she could ever remember. How could it all have gone so wrong? Perhaps she had been pushing her luck getting her mother to write, or rather sign, a cheque. William had said the family didn't have as much money as she'd thought. Perhaps they really were in difficulties. Heavens, it was all too horrible to think about. She had always been brought up in a wealthy environment, believing they had enough money to buy anything they wanted.

Sophie came back into the room. 'Right, I'm ready. I'll go and wait for Fred down near the door. Will you be all right?'

'Course I will. Like I said, I'll phone someone soon and we'll go out. Have a nice evening.'

'Thanks. We will.' She left the flat and Bella heard her running down their stairs. With a sigh, she went to look in the fridge. A couple of eggs were the only food in there. It came to something when a Friday night could only supply a couple of boiled eggs. She went and picked up the phone.

'Charlie,' she said brightly, 'how are you? I was wondering if you're doing anything this evening.'

'Bella, darling. Sorry, but I've got work to do. Boring but necessary. In fact, I should have left half an hour ago. Bye, sorry.' He put the phone down. She gave a shrug and dialled another number.

'Robin, how are you?'

'Got a foul cold. I feel like death warmed up.'

'Oh dear, I am sorry. I won't ask you if you'd like to go out. You sound as if you need to be in bed.'

'I am in bed, as a matter of fact.'

'Okay then. Hope you're soon better. Bye.' Two down; how many left to go? she wondered.

Two more calls gave her similar results, at which point she gave up and went and put the eggs on to boil. By ten o'clock she went to bed, feeling as if her world was ending. She heard Sophie come in sometime later and stayed where she was. She didn't want to hear about her wonderful evening and what a wonderful man Fred was. Fred, she thought. What a boring name for a boring man. She turned over and tried to go to sleep.

11

At Cobridge House, things had moved on quickly. With the decision to move agreed, William had contacted several estate agents, who had sent brochures and lists of properties for sale. They had agreed that they would look for a bungalow, and this morning several sheets of details had been sent to them. At breakfast they were all poring over them.

'This one looks nice,' William said. 'Not far from the park, and a decent size. How many bedrooms do you think we might need?'

'I'd have thought four,' Paula told him. 'One for each of the girls when they want to come, and one each for us and Nellie.'

'This one won't do then. Only three rooms.'

'You do agree with me, don't you? I

don't want to be the one to put a black mark against something we'd possibly like.'

'Yes, I do. We don't want to downgrade so much that we feel closed in.'

They went through everything they'd been sent and chose a couple of places to go and look around.

'I'll call the agents and set up visits,' William said. 'And on Monday I'll call the people who wanted to buy this place. I didn't think it was all going to happen quite so quickly.'

'I suppose I was the fly in the ointment, wasn't I?' Nellie suggested.

'Well, maybe just a bit,' Paula said. 'But you weren't well. Now you're almost back to normal, and it's wonderful.'

'Thank you, dear. I'll admit I do feel better.'

'Do you remember going out that night?' Paula asked her. 'You went near the park.'

'I'm afraid it all seems a bit hazy. It'll be strange living somewhere else. I have to admit, I shall miss this place terribly.

I've lived here for a long time. But we have to move on, don't we?'

'I like the look of this place,' William said, examining one of the sheets from the estate agents. 'It's somewhat larger than we said, but it's lovely. Look, Paula — it's almost perfect.' He passed the sheet over to his wife and she looked at it with interest. It was a five-bedroom bungalow a few miles from where they lived at present.

'It does look lovely,' she agreed. 'But it's a long way from here, near Rough Close. What do you think, Nellie?' She handed the sheet over and Nellie put on her spectacles.

'Yes, dear, it looks nice.'

'What do you think about moving away from here?'

'I suppose I hardly ever go out anywhere these days, so does it really matter? It'd be nearer Joe.'

'Well maybe a little.'

'Are we still having our party?' Nellie asked.

'Perhaps it'll be a farewell party to

this house,' Paula told her. 'Yes, of course we will. Let's get the bungalow settled first. Why not phone them and arrange a visit?'

'I will,' William said. 'In fact, I'll do it right away. It does actually look perfect for us. And at a price we can afford.'

The women sat quietly at the table, waiting for William to return. He came back looking pleased. 'We can go this afternoon,' he told them. 'Three o'clock. The owners are actually away, so the agent will show us round. I have such a good feeling about this. What do you think, Paula?'

'I'm all in favour. Now, I must phone Sophie to make sure my cheque has arrived. I posted it yesterday, so it should be there.'

'Seems like it's changes all round, doesn't it?' said Nellie.

Paula called her daughter and asked about the cheque. Their post had not yet arrived.

'Oh Mum, I don't know what to do. Bella is so down. I feel really guilty about moving. She says she's going to turn over a new leaf. Evidently she's got money problems. She went to the bank yesterday and came back totally defeated. I've never seen her like this before. Do you know anything about it?'

'Well, yes. She got your grandma to sign a cheque and filled in the rest for herself. The account has been closed for the past few weeks.'

'Oh heavens. I suspected it was something like that, but couldn't really believe she'd do it. But it's more than that. She said something about an overdraft. I really don't see how she could get into such a mess. I mean to say, she doesn't ever give me anything towards housekeeping or bills.'

'I don't know. Does she go out a lot?'

'Yes, but usually with some bloke or other.'

'Well perhaps she pays her share.'

'I suppose so. Oh, there's the post now. I'll call you back soon.' Sophie put the phone down and rushed to get the post. Her mother's writing was on one envelope. She tore it open and saw the cheque and a brief note, then dialled home and told her mother it had arrived.

'Thank you so much, Mum. It's very generous of you. I'll keep it till Monday, and if I change my mind over the weekend, I'll send it back to you.'

'Consider it all carefully, dear. Don't be in too much of a hurry either way.'

'I will. I do appreciate it, really I do.' They said their goodbyes and Sophie hung up the phone. Then she took the cheque and put it carefully into her handbag. Soon afterwards, Bella came out of her room.

'What was all that about?'

'All what?'

'The conversation you were having with your mum, I assume.'

'Oh just something she was arranging with me. There's a letter for you by the phone.'

'I don't think I want any more letters.' Bella went and picked it up, then ripped it open and glanced at it.

'Oh, great. The garage want some compensation for getting the car ready for me. Well they can forget it. At least it's now ready for the next person.' She tore it up and threw it into the bin. 'Cheeky so-and-sos.'

'Do you want some breakfast?' Sophie asked her. 'I think there may be enough bread to make toast. I really need to go shopping this morning. There's nothing in the fridge or cupboard.'

'Tell me about it. I'm afraid I had the last two eggs for supper last night.'

'Oh. Well I won't offer you an egg for breakfast, then.'

'Sorry. I was starving, though, and you were out. Did you have a nice time?'

'Yes, thank you. We went to the pictures and then out for supper. Really good evening. You didn't go out, I gather?'

'Nope. Stayed in and watched some drivel on television. Had an early night as a matter of fact.'

* * *

William and Paula were getting ready to go and look at the bungalow when Nellie arrived in the hall wearing her best coat and hat.

'Goodness, Mum, you do look smart,' William said. 'Put us to shame.'

'No use going looking untidy. We want them to see us at our best. Where's your tie, dear?'

'I wasn't going to bother,' replied William uncomfortably.

'Don't be silly. You need to look your best. We don't want them thinking we can't afford to buy the place, now, do we?'

'Mum, we're only going to meet the estate agent, for goodness sake. No one else. The owners are away, if you remember.'

'All the same, I feel it's important to look the part.'

'Well, I'm not wearing a hat for anybody,' said Paula. 'Shall we go?'

It was a reasonable drive from their

house to the new one. William found it easily and pulled into the spacious drive. The estate agent hadn't yet arrived, so they got out of the car and wandered round, looking at the shrubbery. It seemed well-planted with a proliferation of different types of shrubs. It would be relatively easy to maintain, William was thinking. Perhaps they might even find a gardener at a reasonable cost. He looked over the gate at the common. It was a green space, and he knew he could live there.

'What do you think, ladies?' he asked the others.

'Looks quite nice from the outside,' Paula answered. 'I like the common being so near. Perhaps we might get a dog. Be nice to walk over there.'

'I think we need to see the house first, Paula. Ah, this looks like him,' William said as a car drew up.

'I'm so sorry to be late,' the estate agent apologised. 'Someone came into the office at the last minute. Now, I'll just get the keys and we can take a look inside.'

* * *

An hour later they had examined every corner of the place, asked loads of questions, looked over the garden, and felt they had seen everything they needed.

'We'll discuss it at home,' said William to the agent. 'I'll give you a call on Monday to let you know what we think.'

'Thank you very much. I hope you like it. I won't ask you any questions now; I'll leave you to your thoughts.'

'Thank you for showing us round,' Paula told him. 'Kind of you.'

'All part of my job. I'll look forward to hearing from you.'

They all drove away. Paula could hardly contain herself. 'I think it's perfect. A lovely kitchen, and that sunroom was gorgeous. What did you think, Nellie?'

'Oh, it's nice enough. I really will miss Cobridge House, though.'

'But it's too big for us,' William said. 'We're rattling round in there, Mum.

Half the place is shut off. We need to be sensible.'

'I know, dear. We really need to move. But you can't blame me for missing it. You must do as you think fit and not worry about me and my thoughts.'

'That's very generous of you,' Paula said.

Nellie smiled but didn't say any more. They needed to make the decision themselves.

'It is the first property we've considered,' said William.

'If it's right for us, does that matter?' Paula asked him.

'I suppose not. I would like to see what else is around, though.'

'But suppose we lose this one?'

'I doubt that will happen. The agents always say there's a lot of interest anywhere. They want to make a sale as quickly as possible. No, I really want to wait for a while.'

Paula pulled a face but said no more. This was the only place she'd seen that interested her from the pile of details that had arrived in the mail.

'That didn't seem too far,' she said when they arrived back at Cobridge House. Nellie sighed. 'What is it, Nellie?' she asked.

'Oh, nothing. It just seems a bit inevitable. Moving from a place you've known most of your life is rather traumatic. I think I might go and rest for a while.' She went up to her room and shut the door.

'Oh dear, I was afraid this might happen,' William said, concerned. 'It's going to be difficult when we do actually move.'

'But we do have to move, don't we?' Paula pressed him. 'It's foolish to keep this place with all the empty rooms, and short of taking in lodgers, there's no way we can afford to keep it.'

'Perhaps we should advertise our flat. If we had lodgers, it might make a bit of a difference.'

'And you wouldn't mind people sharing the stairs and coming in at all hours? I'm sorry, but it sounds awful to me.'

'Perhaps you're right,' William sighed. 'We never really did sort out that part of it. We'll contact some more estate agents and see what they have to offer. But I don't want to contact them until we've found somewhere to move to.'

'If you must. I doubt we'll find anywhere we like more.'

'Okay, I know you liked the place at Rough Close. We'll have another look at it later in the week.'

He went to his study and closed the door. Paula gave a shrug and started to prepare supper. It seemed like a long time till Monday and any more property details coming in through the mail.

* * *

In Leicester, Bella seemed a changed person. She offered to vacuum the flat and tried to help prepare the food. By the end of Sunday, Sophie was ready to scream. She felt sick of picking up things Bella hadn't done quite as expected and finding her always in the way in the tiny kitchen. But it did make her think twice about moving out to be on her own. She knew how upset Bella would be by the change in her own life, and had almost decided by Monday to send the cheque back to her mother. She decided to speak to Bella about the issue, for better or for worse.

'Can we talk for a minute?' Sophie asked her aunt.

'I thought we'd been talking all day,' Bella laughed.

'You overheard a bit of what I was saying to Mum on the phone.'

'Didn't make any sense to me, but go on.'

'She's sent me a cheque to buy my own flat.'

'What?' exclaimed Bella. 'Why on earth do you want another flat?'

'To be on my own.'

'Don't be silly. You'd be horribly lonely. What would you do without me to keep you on the straight and narrow?'

'Oh yes, and how often do you do that?'

'Don't be silly. I'm here most of the time.'

'But you always expect me to cook for you and do all the shopping,' Paula explained. 'You never offer to pay for anything. You're always going out with someone and expect me to cover for you the next day if you've got a hangover. Just some of the reasons I'm thinking of moving.'

'That's a bit unfair of you. Admittedly, I'm pretty broke at the moment. But I've helped you this weekend, haven't I? I've tried very hard.'

'And how often does this happen?'

'I'm sure you're exaggerating,' Bella said with a shrug. 'And as for cooking, well I'm pretty hopeless. If you're cooking for yourself, it's surely no more trouble to cook for me as well.'

'It's the principle of the thing. If you paid for your share, we might eat better. Not so much mince and so on.'

'Once I'm sorted with the bank, I promise to pay you.'

'Maybe. But you'll doubtless forget

and want to leave it till the next week.'

'You don't have much of an opinion of me, do you?' Sophie said nothing and looked away. 'I'm sorry. I realise I've been a pain. Please don't move away. I promise I'll try my best not to be.'

'I'll think about it.'

'Where were you going to move, anyway?'

'A new block of flats. One near where Fred lives.'

'Oh, him. You've been going out with him, haven't you?'

'Yes, a few times. Nothing to it yet, of course.'

'Yet? You think there might be?'

Sophie blushed. 'Maybe. I do like him quite a lot.'

'So is that why you want a flat near his?'

'No, not at all. It's just that he'd moved into the block of flats and told me there were still some left. Mum and Dad came down on Thursday to have a look.'

'Wow, you're a dark horse. You didn't mention it to me.'

'Well, no. You were at work, anyway, and I took the day off. It was quite difficult not telling you about it all, actually. But they did only come for the day, as Grandma was with them and they didn't want to be out for too long. She's evidently much better. They think it was some sort of infection that was causing her to present with a sort of dementia. I'm not saying she's normal, but she's certainly much better. In only a few days, too.'

'I do feel bad about what I tried to do,' Bella said quietly. 'I suppose I hadn't realised they really are so hard up. Hang on a minute — how come your mother's sent you a cheque for a whole flat? I mean, if they're broke, how can she do that?'

'Her mother left it to her. It's the money from selling her house.'

'Lucky you. What's on the box this evening?'

'*That's Life*, I think.'

'Suppose I might as well watch it. Nothing better to do with myself.'

'Aren't you going out somewhere?'

'Not tonight. Or for the next few nights, I guess. No, it's time I got used to boring television again.'

'Oh dear, you do sound in a bad way. Perhaps things aren't as bleak as they seem.'

'I'm not sure they're not a great deal worse. I think I've completely blotted my copybook at home. I'm short of cash, and don't look like clearing that debt for many months. And now you say you're moving out. Great day it's been.'

'Perhaps I won't move after all.'

'You should go if you want to. Don't mind me. I'm just a misery at the moment. Once I pick myself up again, it'll be all right.'

Sophie looked at her aunt, who was clearly miserable. She couldn't bear to think of Bella struggling so much on her own. If she really did keep her promise to behave differently, perhaps there was no point in moving. Sophie decided there and then that she would wait a while before deciding whether or not to move, and she would keep her mother's cheque in case things didn't work out. If she lost the flat she'd seen, well it wouldn't be so bad. There were other places coming up all the time.

12

Paula was surprised by the amount of mail that arrived the following morning. 'Goodness. We don't usually get this much on a Monday.'

'I contacted more estate agents and they've come up trumps,' William announced. 'Let's start opening them.'

'I'll clear away breakfast first. Then we'll have some space.'

But William had already begun to rip open the envelopes. Paula dumped the dirty things into the sink and sat down again, picking up another heap of papers. She shuffled through them. 'Whatever did you ask for, William? This is a small castle. Quite unsuitable. And this one is a tiny cottage.'

'I told them what we needed. I expect they've sent everything on their books. Throw the unsuitable ones away. I'll get the bin and you can put them into that.

Actually, let me look at the place you call a castle. It might do for us after all.'

'No thanks. I'd rather stay here,' she laughed.

They whittled the pile down to about four places, and then down to two.

'I don't think they're a patch on the place we saw on Saturday,' William said, 'but we might as well give them a once-over. There should be more papers arriving tomorrow too.'

'I don't think they're as good as the Saturday place either. I really liked that one.'

'Some of these are much cheaper.'

'But if they need a lot of work, we won't save anything.'

'I still want to look at them.' William was adamant.

'Okay, arrange to visit. The sooner the better. We don't want to risk losing the other place.'

William went to phone the agents and arrange the visits. 'Right,' he said, 'we visit this one near Newcastle this morning, and the other — well, he's trying to get us there this afternoon. He'll call back in a while when he's spoken to the sellers.'

The phone rang. 'Ah, that didn't take long.' He went to answer it. When he came back, he looked troubled. 'They've had an offer on the Rough Close place.'

'Oh, no. I said we should make up our minds quickly. Oh dear, that's a real blow.'

'We could make a better offer for it. It wasn't for the full price. The offer, I mean. Let's look at the new places first and then decide.'

'We can afford to make a full-price offer, can't we?'

'Of course we can, even before we sell this place. But I want to see what the market has to offer first.'

'I don't know what you think you're going to find, dear. But okay, we'll go and visit the other places. I think the phone's ringing again.'

'Exciting, isn't it?'

'You could call it that,' Paula said. 'I call it rather worrying.'

Nellie came into the room. 'Oh dear, have I missed breakfast?' she asked.

'We had a lot of details from the estate agents come in and wanted to clear the table,' Paula told her. 'I'll make you some toast and tea. Sit down there.'

'Thank you, dear. So where are you looking today? I liked that place we saw yesterday — or Saturday, rather. If we've got to move, it's as good as anywhere.'

'I totally agree,' Paula said. She told her mother-in-law about the offer they'd had and that William wanted to see more places.

'Silly boy. Why look any further? He needs to get in with a better offer, and quickly.'

Paula nodded. 'There you are. Toast. Tea won't be a minute. It's just brewing.'

'Right,' said William, coming back into the room. 'The second place, well, we can't go round till tomorrow, so I've said forget it. Hope that's all right with you, dear?'

'Course it is,' Paula answered.

'Oh morning, Mother,' William greeted Nellie.

'Morning, dear. I can't think why you want to bother with anywhere else. Nothing wrong with the place we saw on Saturday. I quite liked it.'

'You weren't very enthusiastic then.'

'Well I've had time to think about it. If we've got to move, it might as well be to somewhere like that.'

'Well yes, but I want to see this place today,' William insisted. 'It's a lot cheaper than the bungalow.'

They all set off later, Nellie again sporting her hat. It wasn't as easy to find this place, and when they did, they were rather late. The agent was waiting in his car, looking slightly cross. He leapt out as they stopped.

'Sorry,' William apologised. 'Couldn't see which place it was.'

'No worries, sir.' He shook hands with them all, and Paula winced at the smell of a rather over-enthusiastic dose of aftershave. 'Come on in. The owner's

233

wife is here but she won't mind us looking round. Follow me.' He pushed open the door and went inside.

'This is the hall, of course. Notice the solid wood panelling and doors to the various rooms. Here we have the lounge.' He opened the door and showed them inside. It was a pleasant enough room but rather small, Paula thought. Next was the dining room. Again, a rather small room, and one which would never house their large dining table. The kitchen was next. This was a reasonable size and fairly modern. There was still no sign of the owner's wife, so no opportunity for questions.

'We'll go look at the bedrooms next. Can I offer you some assistance up the stairs?' the agent asked Nellie.

'No, thank you. I'll stay down here and let you go. I wanted a bungalow.'

'I think perhaps we'll give the rest a miss,' said William, looking at his wife for agreement.

'It really isn't what we're looking for,' Paula told the agent. 'Thank you for your time, but I think we'll leave it.'

'Are you sure? There are some nice rooms upstairs.' William shook his head. 'If you're really sure.' The agent looked rather deflated.

'Sorry,' Paula said as they were leaving. 'Well, that was a waste of time,' she added as they drove away. 'Can't we make an offer on Rough Close?'

'I suppose so,' William answered. 'Do you want to go and take another look at it first?'

'Not really. We can go and look again when it's ours.'

'You do sound positive about it.'

'I think I am.'

'So am I,' said Nellie. 'It'll be a nice place to end my days.'

'Don't talk like that, Mum,' William insisted. 'Your life isn't over yet. You might even meet someone else and get married again.'

'Don't be ridiculous. Let's get home now. I'd kill for a coffee.'

★ ★ ★

By the time they were having their evening meal, they were the proud owners of a bungalow. William had made his offer, which was accepted, and he had contacted the company that was interested in buying Cobridge House. He was going to hold out for the best price he could get and threatened to call an estate agent to sell it.

'Don't do that, sir,' the owner of the company had begged. 'We'll make you a better deal than any agent.' And it was settled.

'Shall I call Sophie and tell them about the bungalow?' Paula asked.

'If you want to, dear,' William said.

She could hardly wait to tell her daughter the news as she picked up the phone and dialled. When Sophie answered, she told her, 'We've made an offer for the bungalow that's been accepted. It's very exciting. I think you'll love it. Now, have you made an offer for your flat?'

'Well, no, Mum. If it's okay, I'll hang onto your cheque until I've decided. Bella's here and I've told her my plans.

She wasn't very happy.'

'Oh dear. I assume she's listening to what you're saying?'

'Yes, she is.'

'Is she behaving any better?'

'Absolutely.'

'And that's why you're planning to stay?'

'Yes, pretty much.'

'You hang on to the cheque for a while, then. If she falls back into her usual habits, you'll still be able to move.'

'OK, Mum, if you're sure. Thanks a lot. I really hope you'll be happy in your new place. When do you think you'll be moving?'

'Possibly in a couple of months or so.'

'How exciting. I'll book some holiday when you know and come and help you.'

They chatted for a while and eventually said their goodbyes. Bella asked what was going on.

'They've made an offer on a bunga-low at Rough Close. It's been accepted, so they'll be moving in about two months.'

'That's nice for them. Will Mum go with them?'

'Yes, of course. And there are rooms for both of us, too.'

'Really? I should have thought they'd forget about me, after what I did. And I gather you've decided against moving?'

'For a while, anyway. Depends on . . .'

'How I behave.'

'Well, yes.'

'I'm going to turn over a new leaf. I'll be a perfect flatmate from now on.'

'Yes, well, we'll see.'

★   ★   ★

The next few weeks at Cobridge House were rather hectic. The three of them had so much furniture to part with, it was going to take a while to get rid of. Paula was rushing round with lists of things they wanted to sell and lists of things to keep. It was the huge, long, glass-fronted display unit that was giving her nightmares. Would it fit into their new lounge, or would they have to sell it? She really wanted to keep it as something the family had created over all their years of making china. Even the china itself was going to be a huge problem to pack, but they were leaving it for a while so that when the family came for the promised party, it didn't look empty and a mess.

It had been Nellie who reminded her about the family party. With all the excitement of moving, Paula had forgotten all about it. She wasn't sure how she would have time to do all the cooking, but William advised her to buy pre-prepared food.

'Really?' she said, delighted at the prospect. She started making more lists of things to buy.

'You'll turn yourself into a list if you're not careful,' William teased her. 'Do you think we should keep the cupboard in the spare bedroom?'

'I can't think of anything else at the

moment. Why don't you go and phone your various aunts and uncles and invite them to the party?'

'Okay. A week on Saturday, you said?'

'Yes. Afternoon only. I can't do lunch for that lot.'

William went off to his study and made his own list. Then he started to call the family.

'That's terrific,' Lizzie commented. 'Are you including the children? Don't know why I still call them children. Heavens, they're nearly old enough to have kids of their own.'

'Yes, of course,' he said. 'Bring them all.'

'There are only two of them. It just seems like more. We'll be there, all right.'

William ticked them off on his list and then called Joe, who was delighted to hear their news.

'You'll be much nearer to us when you move. Are the kids invited to your party?'

'Course,' said William. 'Can't leave them out.'

More ticks on his list. He called Billy and got the same result; he wanted to bring his children too. William went to find Paula.

'Everyone wants to come,' he said with a smile. 'And they all want to bring their children, so I said yes. I know it means a few extras, but if you're buying everything in, it won't matter, will it?'

'Billy's two are both married with kids of their own. I did say it would have to be the adults only.'

'But the kids are now all adults. Everyone has got older.'

'I suppose so,' Paula sighed. 'And have you invited our daughter? And Bella?'

'Thought I'd leave that to you. I know how much you enjoy speaking to Sophie.'

'Is Bella to be included?'

'Not sure. After what she did to Mum . . . '

'I think Nellie would be upset if she was missed out. I'll speak to Sophie later and invite them both. We can't go on punishing Bella forever. Besides, she's improved no end lately, according to Sophie.'

'Whatever you think. And don't worry about the cost of ordering things. We shall make a good deal on this place, and you'll probably be able to have someone come to clean in the new place. I've also decided to find a job of some sort, even if it's only as a part-time barman or something. This is going to be the start of a new phase in my life.'

'Goodness me, it *is* a new start. This party will be our grand finale. A chance for everyone to say goodbye to Cobridge House.'

'They'll all want to come to the new place. We'll have to have another party to celebrate our housewarming, I expect.'

'I'll drop off the order at the butcher's tomorrow,' Paula said, her tone becoming business-like. 'There'll still be a lot for me to do even if the food is ordered. Still, I shall probably enjoy it.'

'I'm sorry it's all for my half of the family. Isn't there anyone from your family we can invite?'

'No, I don't really have anyone left after Mum and Auntie Wyn died. Not to worry, though. I've always got Sophie on my side.'

When she phoned her daughter, she was out. Bella answered the phone and Paula was surprised. 'Oh, Bella. Where's Sophie?'

'Out with Fred, I think. They seem quite close these days. Can I pass on a message?'

'Well yes, but I was going to ask you too. We're having a farewell party to Cobridge House a week on Saturday. We do hope you'll both be there with us. If you tell Sophie, I'll phone her later in the week to make sure. Will you come?'

'Are you sure you want me? I mean, how will Mum take it if I'm there?'

'I think she would much rather you were here than on your own in Leicester. Please do come.'

'I'll try,' Bella said. 'If you're sure.'

'I am. So how's it going? At work I mean.'

'Not too bad. I expect Sophie's told

you she's been promoted?'

'No, she hasn't mentioned it.'

'She's actually designing stuff now instead of being my assistant. She's talented, I have to admit. She did one evening dress and said it was mine. When the boss found out, he promoted her immediately.'

'That's good. Well I suppose it wasn't so good for you.'

'I've realised what a pain I've been,' Bella said in an apologetic tone. 'No more, though. I'm a reformed character.'

'Glad to hear it. We shall look forward to seeing you next week. Bye, now.'

Paula took great pleasure in telling William and Nellie about her call and about Bella's reformation.

'So how did she seem?' asked Nellie.

'I thought she seemed much quieter than before. I know she's very sorry for trying to con us — well, you — out of the money. And Sophie's seeing much more of Fred. I think it's quite serious, actually.'

'I was thinking that when we move

and have sold this place, I'd quite like to buy a car for the two of them,' William suggested. 'What do you think, Paula?'

'I think it's a lovely idea, don't you, Nellie?'

'I'm not sure she deserves it.'

'Maybe not,' William said, 'but I think it would be a nice gesture. Nothing too fancy. Perhaps you could give them your old car, Paula, and you can have a new one.'

'Now that's a very good idea,' she agreed with a smile. 'I think that would solve the problem completely.'

'You spoil them,' Nellie said. 'Bella is only your sister, you know, William. It's not as if she's your daughter or something.'

'I'll think about it. After the last visit, I thought I'd never want to see her again. But I've changed my mind, I believe.'

'Well, I'm glad about that,' Paula replied. 'There's nothing worse than family feuds. Not that I'd blame you, of course.'

She continued with her lists for the

rest of the evening. She had orders for the butcher's shop and the bakery, and she wanted to ask the latter if they would make a fruitcake too. The greengrocer would provide salad things and fruit for a trifle. She'd still have lots to do around the event, and with Bella and Sophie arriving on the Friday evening she would need to make something more special for dinner. Heavens, it was going to be such a lot of work. Paula gritted her teeth and told herself she would enjoy every minute of it, then went back to her lists.

13

The day before the party, Nellie was being a pain to Paula, constantly asking about the food and what she could wear.

'I wondered about getting a new dress for the party,' Nellie said to her. 'Something a bit more modern. What do you think, dear?'

'I'm sorry, but unless William can take you out, I'm far too busy. This isn't like the old days, you realise. I'm having to do it all myself.'

'All right then, dear, give me a job. There must be something I can do.'

'You could lay the table for dinner this evening. Bella and Sophie will be here, so lay for five.'

'I can do that. It's bit early, though, isn't it?'

'Well maybe, but if you're willing, it's a job out of the way.'

Paula sighed as she left the room. She consulted her lists once more. 'Oh heavens, I haven't made the trifles,' she muttered. There would be at least twenty guests coming tomorrow and she felt rather nervous about catering for so many. She put the sponges to soak and chopped up fruit to put on top. She worked hard for the rest of the day. Before she knew where she was, it was time to collect Sophie and Bella from the station.

'William,' Paula called, 'time to get the girls. Can you go, please? William —?' But there was no sign of her husband. She rushed upstairs to his study and then looked in all the other rooms, but he seemed to have disappeared. Where on earth was he? The car was still outside, so she knew he must be around. She looked at her watch again. If he didn't go soon, Sophie and Bella would be left standing on the platform. She tugged off her apron, told Nellie she was going out, and turned the heat off from under the vegetables.

Then she drove to the station, which took her over twenty minutes, and arrived at the same time as the train.

'Hello,' she called. 'Over here, Sophie, Bella.'

'Hallo, Mum,' Sophie greeted her. 'We were expecting Dad to collect us.'

'So was I. He seems to have disappeared, so I came instead. The car's over here. How are you both?'

They chatted all the way home, Sophie telling her mother about her new job. Bella seemed somewhat subdued, Paula thought. Possibly she was dreading seeing her mother again.

When they arrived home, William came to greet them. 'I'm so sorry, dear. I was up in one of the servants' rooms and quite forgot the time. Anyway, I'm glad you were able to go and collect them. How are you both?'

★ ★ ★

The evening went well, and Bella, it seemed, was quite forgiven for her

249

attempts to cheat her mother. When William told her and Sophie about his plans to pass on Paula's car to them, they were both delighted.

'That's terrific of you, Dad!' Sophie exclaimed. 'It'll be lovely not to have to rely on buses.'

'And we can drive home sometimes, too,' Bella added. 'Thanks very much, William. And you, too, Paula.'

'Not sure how soon it will be,' William said. 'We have the move to think about first, but after that we shall look at a new car for Paula.'

Bella muttered something but then stopped. Paula guessed what she was thinking but said nothing.

'So, how are the plans for tomorrow's bash?' Bella asked.

'Okay, I think,' Paula replied. 'I still have quite a bit to do. Did you organise the wine and beer, William? Oh and we should have some sherry for the ladies, don't you think?'

'I'll go out tomorrow and get it,' he offered. 'Tell me what you want and I'll go round to the off-licence.'

'You mean you haven't got it yet?' Paula said, irritated. 'Really, William. Then get what you think you'll need. They are your family, after all.'

William looked suitably contrite. 'Can you remember what you used to have, Mum?' he asked Nellie.

'Course I can't. James always took care of that side of things. And I never did go and buy a new dress for the occasion.'

'You've got lots of nice things, Mum,' Bella said. 'We'll look after supper and see what we can find, shall we?' Nellie nodded her agreement.

'So, who's coming tomorrow?' asked Sophie.

'Everyone, it seems,' Paula answered.

'What, all the children too?'

'Your father said it'd be all right if they all came. It'll have to be a buffet sort of tea. No way can we all sit round the table.'

'It won't seem the same,' wailed Nellie. 'We always sat round the table

251

when your father and I had tea parties.'

'I think everyone's had too many children,' William said. 'And their children have got children too. Billie's two boys have both two of their own. How about Joe's daughter? Hasn't she got a child?' He was busily adding up everyone who'd be there.

'Let's have pudding now,' Paula said. 'If you can clear away the vegetable dishes, Sophie, I'll take the plates.'

* * *

At last it was bedtime, and Paula sank down into a chair, feeling exhausted. Her mind was still racing through lists, and she wondered if there would be enough food. Perhaps she'd send William out to get more bread and maybe some pork pies to add to the feast. She did want it all to be a success, for Nellie's sake.

At last she fell asleep, troubled by dreams of crowds of people turning up with nothing ready for them. She woke early and went downstairs to the kitchen. She sat looking at her lists and drinking hot tea.

Nellie came in to join her. 'I really do appreciate you doing all this, you know,' she said. 'It's very good of you, especially as you have no help at all. I just wanted to say I'll help as much as I can, and try not to make extra demands on you.'

'Oh Nellie, thank you so much. I'm looking forward to it, or I will be when everything's ready. I'm going to slice the ham next. It'll keep in the fridge. Then it's salads to get ready. Sorry, I'm getting carried away.'

'I'll make some toast, shall I?' Nellie offered.

'Thank you. If you can manage it.'

'I think I can just about do that.' Nellie smiled. 'This sliced bread makes life so much easier, doesn't it? Goodness, I don't know what Wyn would have made of it all. And Cook would have gone mad. She always used to make her own bread.'

Nellie chattered on as she made the toast and sat eating it. Paula loved listening to her talk about the past, and ate her own toast as she worked. At last Sophie and Bella came down, along with William.

'I'm in charge of toast today,' said Nellie proudly. 'Bella, you make a fresh pot of tea, and Sophie, get the cups and plates sorted.'

Paula smiled to herself. This was Nellie as she'd first known her.

At last it was time to get ready. The table was laid and some of the food was put out. Wine and beer were sitting to one side and chairs were set round the edge of the room. Paula knew there would never be enough, but everyone could stand around talking, or so she hoped. Nellie was bright as a button, wearing one of her best dresses which Bella had dug out of her wardrobe. Paula was wearing one of her best dresses too; and Sophie was wearing something she had made herself, while Bella had donned a long Laura Ashley dress. Even William had done well, wearing one of his suits and a smart tie.

'You all look a credit to us,' Nellie said cheerfully. 'Oh, I think I hear someone coming.'

Lizzie and Daniel were the first to arrive. 'How lovely of you to invite us all,' Lizzie said brightly. 'The boys are coming under their own steam. I hope it's okay, but Daniel Two wanted to bring his latest flame. I think he's serious about this one, but you can never tell with him.'

'It's a buffet anyway,' Paula told her, 'so no worries about extras. William said everyone wanted to come. It'll be a bit of a finale here at Cobridge House. We shall be moving in two weeks. Oh, here are Joe and Daisy. And Sally and her husband. And who's the young man with them?' Paula frowned.

'Hiya,' Joe said. 'This is Sam, our grandson.'

'Goodness me, how enormous these young men are!' Paula exclaimed. 'Welcome, Sam, and Sally, Daisy, and

Joe. Come on in and get a drink.'

They all exchanged kisses and hugs. Everyone seemed pleased to have the chance to see each other, and Paula stood back, leaving them all to chatter. There was just Billy and his party to arrive and everyone would be there. The noise level was already becoming as much as she could stand, so Paula slipped into the kitchen to check on anything she could think of. She filled two large old kettles and put them on a low heat. Then Sophie joined her.

'What are you doing, Mum?'

'Just getting away from the noise for a few minutes. Has Billy arrived yet?'

'Yes, they've all just come in. I didn't know both his boys had got two babies each. Well, two little ones each.' There was a sudden small-child yell.

'I suppose I should go and see what that was all about,' Paula said.

Sophie put her hand on her mother's shoulder. 'I should let them sort it out. You've done a really good job here. A lovely meal for everyone, and well, I think you're a miracle worker. Come on, let's go and greet the newcomers.' She tucked her hand under Paula's arm and together they went to greet Billy and Jenny.

Paula looked around the assembled crowd and smiled. Nellie was sitting in the midst of her brothers and sisters, looking happier than she had for ages.

'And you should see the new place we're moving to,' she was telling them. 'It's beautiful, and so modern. The kitchen's a perfect dream — isn't it, Paula?'

'Oh, it certainly is. But you'll all have to come over and see it for yourselves.'

'We shall have to get settled in first, of course,' Nellie told them. 'But you'll all be made welcome.'

'I think it's an excellent idea,' Lizzie enthused. 'We've been saying for ages this place is too large for you now, haven't we, Daniel?'

'If you're ready to eat, do come into the dining room,' Paula invited them all. She watched as they fell upon the food and carried filled plates away with them. Nellie stopped beside her.

'You've done us proud, Paula. Thank you. I won't ever forget today. Having everyone here together . . . well, it means so much. We're quite a family, aren't we?'

'We certainly are. Thanks, Nellie. I appreciate your comments.'

'Mum,' said Sophie softly, 'I know it isn't really the time, but is it all right if Fred comes over tomorrow? I really want you to meet him, and he wants to meet you too.'

'Of course it is, dear. He should have come today, and he could have met all the family.'

'I think that might have been a bit much. Tomorrow he can meet you and Dad and Grandma. I know I shouldn't really tell you, but he's asked me to marry him.'

'Oh Sophie, my darling!' Paula gasped. 'That's wonderful. Have you said yes?'

'Not until he's met you two. But I really do want to marry him.'

'This is turning into quite a weekend,' Paula breathed. 'My little girl getting married. I can't believe it.'

She stood by the cooker and smiled fit to burst. She could hardly wait for the next stage in her life.

WHERE THE HEART IS
OUT OF THE BLUE
TOMORROW'S DREAMS
DARE TO LOVE
WHERE LOVE BELONGS
TO LOVE AGAIN
DESTINY CALLING
THE SURGEON'S MISTAKE
GETTING A LIFE
ONWARD AND UPWARD
THE DAIRY

We do hope that you have enjoyed reading this large print book.

Did you know that all of our titles are available for purchase?

We publish a wide range of high quality large print books including:
Romances, Mysteries, Classics
General Fiction
Non Fiction and Westerns

Special interest titles available in large print are:
The Little Oxford Dictionary
Music Book, Song Book
Hymn Book, Service Book

Also available from us courtesy of Oxford University Press:
Young Readers' Dictionary
(large print edition)
Young Readers' Thesaurus
(large print edition)

For further information or a free brochure, please contact us at:
Ulverscroft Large Print Books Ltd.,
The Green, Bradgate Road, Anstey,
Leicester, LE7 7FU, England.
Tel: (00 44) **0116 236 4325**
Fax: (00 44) **0116 234 0205**

LUCY OF LARKHILL

Christina Green

Lucy is left to run her Dartmoor farm virtually on her own after a hired hand is injured. She does her best to carry on; though when she decides to sell her baked goods direct to the public, she is forced to admit that she is overwhelmed. She needs to hire a man to help on the farm, and her childhood friend Stephen might just be the answer. But as Lucy's feelings for him grow, she is more determined than ever to remain an independent spinster . . .

FINDING HER PERFECT FAMILY

Carol MacLean

Fleeing as far as she can from an unhappy home life, Amelia Knight arrives at the tropical island of Trinita to work as a nanny at the Grenville estate. As she battles insects and tropical heat, she must also fight her increasing attraction to baby Lucio's widowed father, Leo Grenville — a man whose heart has been broken, and thus is determined never to love again. Amelia must conquer stormy weather and reveal a desperate secret before she can find her perfect family to love forever.

THE SAPPHIRE

Fay Cunningham

Cass, a talented jeweller, wants a quiet life after having helped to solve a murder case. But life is anything but dull while she lives with her mother, an eccentric witch with a penchant for attracting trouble. Now Cass's father, who left the family when she was five, is back on the scene — as well handsome detective Noel Raven, with whom Cass has an electrifying relationship. As dangers both worldly and paranormal threaten Cass and those she loves, will they be strong enough to stand together and prevail?

TROUBLE IN PARADISE

Susan Udy

When Kat's mother, Ruth, tells her that her home and shop are under threat of demolition from wealthy developer Sylvester Jordan, Kat resolves to support her struggle to stay put. So when a mysterious vandal begins to target the shop, Sylvester — or someone in his employ — is their chief suspect. However, Sylvester is also offering Kat opportunities that will support her struggling catering business — and, worst of all, she finds that the attraction she felt to him in her school days is still very much alive . . .